# SINS OF THE FATHER

# SINS OF THE FATHER

MIA COUNTS LYNCH

# Contents

*For my grandmother, who inspired my love of history.*

# Prologue

*"To surrender dreams – this may be madness." -*
*Miguel de Cervantes, Don Quixote*

It was Andrea's favorite story. The beautiful young woman falling in love with the dashing *conquistador*. Theirs was a star-crossed love; she was a Mayan, part of the land for hundreds of years before the Spaniards even knew where to look. He was a member of the nobility, hoping to honor his family by bringing back the riches of the New World home to Spain. Little did he know, but the real riches of the land were the people.

Don Ademar Reynaldo de Piña belonged to a fine old family, admired for its bravery and ties to the Spanish Crown. Don Ademar planned to earn gold and elevate his position in Court through his part of the conquest of New Spain - he found gold and silver and great wealth, but he also found himself in love.

Itzel was a simple girl who knew nothing of riches. Her family lived simply in a thatch-roofed house, in a *pueblo* outside the newly Spanish city of Mérida. She remembered before the Spaniards arrived, of course, but the Mayans were mostly left alone until one day Don Ademar rode into her pueblo with other

Spaniards looking to hire workers to build a church in the city center. He saw her smiling face and was lost.

It could have been cliché, or it could have just been how Itzel told the story, but it took no time at all for the young couple to fall in love. They would sneak away from the pueblo and the city so they could be alone, together. When it was the two of them, Ademar and Itzel could simply be a man and a woman, not a Spaniard and a Mayan, and not a nobleman and a peasant. Neither could speak the other's language, but what could be more common than the language of love? They spoke in caresses and light touches, in tender looks and murmured whispers of devotion. They fell in love under the open blue skies, far away from kings and queens, without a thought for the future.

It was simple until it was no longer possible to ignore their differences. Ademar was recalled to Spain to take his place as head of the Piña family, while Itzel remained in New Spain, left behind with a daughter named Andrea who was part of both worlds, but belonged to neither.

\* \* \*

# One

*"Obviously," replied Don Quijote, "you don't know much about adventures." - Miguel de Cervantes, Don Quixote*

*Mérida, Yucatán 1561*

"You cannot be serious." Andrea Tun looked down at the large certificate in her hands. Her eyes skipped over the tall black flourishes to the circle of red wax at the bottom corner. She had never seen it in person, but every man and woman in New Spain could recognize the seal of the king. She stared at it, fixated.

"I assure you, Doña Andrea, I am quite serious."

The certificate jerked in her hands at the title. It was a joke, it had to be. She was no Doña, she was Andrea Tun. She lived in the rooms above her shop two streets from the *Plaza Mayor* and had lived there all her life. First with her mother Itzel and then, for the past three months, alone.

"But, a *marqués*? Why would she not tell me?"

The man looked at her with pity. He was a secretary for one

of the merchants in Mérida and turned his head to look out the open door of the shop.

"I cannot speak to that, but Don Ademar wishes you to join him in Spain. I will make all the arrangements. The next ship bound for Sevilla leaves in three days. You will leave Mérida tomorrow at 9 o'clock, and will arrive at the port in Veracruz one hour before the *San Martín* departs." He spoke with the knowledge of someone who made the journey often.

"I need more time," Andrea pleaded. "I have not yet decided. There is the store and my family..."

The man sighed, nodding after a moment. "Very well. But you must decide by tonight."

"I will be here at 9 o'clock with a carriage. I hope you will join me." He bowed and walked to the door, pausing when he ducked under the lintel. "Your father hopes you will join me."

Andrea closed the door after him, signaling to all potential customers the shop was closed. Not for the first time, she wished Itzel still lived. Of course, if her mother were alive there would be no question. She would stay here in Mérida, a Maya shop owner. She knew she had some Spanish blood in her, for she fit in among the few Spaniards who did not know her in the city. But everyone knew she was Andrea Tun, so why would that man call her 'Doña'? And why did she now hold a certificate of legitimacy?

Only one person besides Itzel would know, and Andrea was determined to find answers. She would go to her grandmother.

* * *

The pueblo just outside Mérida was like most Mayan pueblos, with dirt roads surrounded by thatched huts and iguanas napping in the sun, and Andrea felt calmer the closer she walked to her grandmother's home. She walked past the familiar women chatting in front of their homes, gossiping while making tortillas. They all looked up at her, calling out greetings. Andrea waved at them knowing it would not take long for them to find out how her life had changed. Their friendly smiles would quickly change to deference when they realized who she was now. She walked quickly into the last hut on the dirt path. It was the home her mother grew up in, the home Itzel and Andrea came to visit every Sunday after Church. As a child, her grandmother would tell stories of the old days, before the Spanish came, tales of gods and heroes.

"*Mamich!*" Andrea called out to her grandmother.

The woman looked up from her work and smiled when she saw Andrea. Her hair had silvered with age and her face was creased and weathered, but she worked with the fervor of a younger woman, pounding *maiz* into flour day in and day out. Andrea was surprised, though not ungrateful, to find her alone.

"Andrea, sit by me," Mamich said, patting the ground next to her.

Andrea sat obediently and took the mortar and pestle from her grandmother. She pounded the maiz, the ache in her muscles a good one.

They sat together in silence, side by side until all of the maiz was ground. She the mortar down next to her, carefully out of the dirt and dust.

"Mamich? Do you know anything about my father?" she asked.

Mamich stiffened. "We made a decision a long time ago never to speak his name."

"But you know who he is?" Andrea insisted.

"Yes, I know," Mamich said reluctantly. "Why are you asking these questions? No good will come out of them."

Andrea reached into her reticule and pulled out the certificate. She unrolled it, careful not to damage the seal. Her grandmother's eyes widened at the sight of it.

"What does it say, Andrea?"

Her grandmother could not understand Spanish, so Andrea translated it as she read it aloud.

*"I hereby declare Doña Andrea de Piña the legitimate daughter of Don Ademar de Piña, Marqués de Benidoleig. Signed, Felipe II, Rey de España, Portugal, Nápoles, Sicilia, Cerdeña, duque de Milán, soberano de los Países Bajos y duque de Borgoña, rey de Inglaterra e Irlanda iure uxoris."*

"When did you get that?" Her grandmother demanded, snatching the certificate out of her hands.

"Today." Andrea carefully pried the certificate away from her grandmother, rolling it back up and putting it in her reticule. "He wants me to live with him in Spain."

She looked at her grandmother, who looked like she had aged ten years. "Mamich?"

Her grandmother reached out her hand and Andrea took it, the delicate bones reminding her that her grandmother was an old woman. She clutched at that beloved hand, blinking back tears.

"I always knew this day would come," her grandmother said. "When my darling Itzel," she gulped, "died and there was no word I thought perhaps I was wrong. Don Ademar is your father. If he has recognized you, you must go to him. You cannot stay here."

"Why not? Nothing needs to change. I have the shop, and my life is here. You are here!"

A tremulous smile appeared on Mamich's face. "Your life has already changed, Andrea. Why do you think your mother gave you a Spanish name? With your light eyes and pale skin, you have always looked like you could be Spanish. Now," she said gesturing to the certificate in the reticule, "you are."

"What if I do not want to be Spanish, Mamich?"

"It does not matter, darling. You are Spanish."

Her grandmother stood. "Now," she said in a tone that brooked no argument, "help me make dinner, and I will take you to say your goodbyes."

Andrea stood outside her shop promptly at 9 o'clock the next morning, her bag at her feet. She took a final glance at the city that had always been her home. She was not ready to say goodbye, but life would not wait until she was ready.

"Courage, Andrea," she whispered as the carriage pulled up in front of her. Spain, and her father, were waiting.

# Two

*"The most perceptive character in a play is the fool, because the man who wishes to seem simple cannot possibly be a simpleton." - Miguel de Cervantes, Don Quixote*

*Sevilla, Spain 1561*

Gabriel was tired of playing the fool. It had been four months since King Felipe had ordered him to investigate a string of cargo losses along the trade route between Spain and New Spain, and three months since he began working with Don Ademar Reynaldo de Piña. As the Marqués de Silva and his father's only son, Gabriel easily integrated himself into Ademar's operation. A few well-placed complaints about being under his father's thumb and Ademar had approached him. From experience, Gabriel knew that all masterminds preferred to think of themselves as the most intelligent in the room, so Gabriel threw himself into the role of lackey with gusto. The novelty of playing a part had since faded, and Gabriel was desperate for something, anything, that would explain the losses.

The king had been more than patient, but that would run out

at some point. Likely sooner rather than later. Ademar did not share all aspects of his business with Gabriel, which meant he needed to do something drastic.

Gabriel was a soldier, an agent of the King. He was used to doing things he would rather not do. Therefore he did what any gentleman would do. He squared his shoulders and knocked on the door.

A thin, reedy voice called, "Come in."

Don Ademar sat behind his desk, the usual mountains of papers piling up on each end. It was a monstrous thing of oak, with elaborately carved legs and spreading so widely it looked like a table. The rest of the study was richly appointed, with expensive furnishings and lush velvet curtains. The carpets were so thick a foot could not feel the floor. Books covered the walls except for a window facing the inner courtyard of the house. A tray with a decanter filled with wine and two glasses sat on a lacquered side table in the between two chairs that sat underneath the windows. Whatever he thought of the man, Gabriel had to admit that Ademar knew how to live nicely.

"Good afternoon, Don Ademar," Gabriel said, walking fully into the study.

Ademar waved him to a seat. "Sit down, sit down. Wine?" he asked, lifting the stopper from the decanter and pouring himself a generous measure of wine.

Gabriel nodded, fixing his character's mask of eagerness to his face. He accepted the glass and sat down with a studied nonchalance.

Ademar returned to the chair behind his desk. He always maintained a deliberate boundary between teacher and pupil when it came to the upper levels of the business, a boundary Gabriel was determined to penetrate.

Taking a sip of the Madeira, Gabriel hid a grimace at its sweetness. He preferred the Armagnac that was making its way throughout Europe from France.

"The taxes from the latest voyage were collected this morning from your warehouse," Gabriel said. "Pedro made sure to tally every last grain of sugar."

Ademar mhmm'd as he searched the left-handed pile on his desk. He pulled out a sheet of paper. It was a list of every item of cargo from the *Santa Ana*, a ship that had just docked in Sevilla from Veracruz. The *Casa de Contratación* collected a twenty percent tax on the goods called the *Quinto Real* on behalf of the king. While Ademar imported every good he could get his hands on, the silver, tobacco, and sugar were particularly good avenues of income. He felt the loss from taxes keenly, and by the richness of his home, had obviously found a way around it.

About two years ago, Don Ademar's legal income decreased while his lifestyle improved. A second son, he had entered the merchant trade and was sent to New Spain as a young man. The death of his elder brother allowed Ademar to return to Spain when he inherited the title. Court expected a marqués to live a certain lifestyle, and Ademar's inheritance allowed for an increase in spending, but it had come to Felipe's attention that he was living beyond his new means.

Gabriel was not a gambler, but he wagered Ademar had resorted to smuggling to maintain his lifestyle. The *Quinto Real* amounted to a great deal of money, tempting for any man let alone one as greedy as Ademar. Gabriel's task was to prevent

Ademar from bypassing the tax, and discover how he was smuggling contraband goods into Spain. So far, Gabriel had only ensured that all goods he knew about were accounted for properly.

Admar was clearly annoyed as he read through the list of cargo the clerk Pedro had sent over earlier in the day.

"Of course," he muttered belatedly, "Pedro is very thorough."

Gabriel smirked, hastily adopting a bland expression with Ademar looked up at him. His green eyes narrowed for a moment upon Gabriel's, before returning to his papers. After a time, Ademar shuffled the papers and put them back into a neat pile. He drank half his wine in one swallow.

"My daughter will be arriving on the *San Martin* in two weeks."

"Your daughter?" Gabriel was rarely, if ever, shocked. But the arrival of a daughter unknown even to the king's advisors was shocking. Don Ademar belonged to his father's generation, and Gabriel had never heard a daughter mentioned before. Indeed, the gossip surrounding the de Piña family centered around the lack of a direct heir because Ademar had never married. "I was unaware you had a daughter, Don Ademar."

"No doubt you were," Ademar laughed. "Nevertheless, she will be here and you will meet her at the port."

Gabriel barely managed to refrain from lifting his eyebrows. Instead, he waved his hand with a flourish. "I would be honored, Don, but -"

"Excellent. She has lived in New Spain all her life so I do not doubt it will be easy to spot her. She will be a bumpkin, but she will be useful."

"Of course, Don Ademar. Are you planning to introduce her to Court then?" Gabriel asked, keeping his voice light.

"Obviously." Ademar's bored eyes suddenly glinted. "The Vizconde Martín is looking for a wife."

The Vizconde Martín was also incredibly wealthy. It suddenly made sense for Ademar to send for this mysterious daughter. The easiest and most legitimate, way to accumulate more money was through marriage.

"Have you ever thought about marrying? I myself may be considering taking a wife," Gabriel mused, although he had not been considering any such thing.

"Pah," Ademar waved his hand as though swatting a fly. "I have no wish for anyone poking their nose into my affairs."

Instead, he was stuck with Gabriel, who suddenly had an idea. He would collect the daughter at the port, and see if she could be of use.

Gabriel drank the rest of his wine and wisely said nothing.

* * *

Andrea never knew where the money came from until her mother died. Her mother Itzel worked hard as a shop owner frequented by the wives of upper Spanish society, but that was not enough to keep Itzel and Andrea in their two-story house with more than one servant. Her pale skin allowed her to go about in town with a small measure of deference from those who did not know her, and her mother bundled her in dresses and unfashionably wide-brimmed hats to protect her skin from darkening in the sun. Her mother's family held her at arm's length, but that did not deter Itzel's desire to see her daughter looking as Spanish as possible. Andrea knew she had a father, of course, but she never dreamed her pale skin was a gift from a high ranking member of the Spanish nobility. One minute she was *Señorita* Andrea, daughter of Itzel, fulfilling orders in her mother's shop. The next minute the friends with whom she had grown up were curtsying to her, calling her *Doña* Andrea de Piña, daughter of Don Ademar Reynaldo de Piña, Spanish conquistador. She held a certificate of legitimacy in one hand and passage booked from New Spain to Spain in the other, and she was suddenly a new person.

She could admit to herself that she was afraid. She was afraid to leave Mérida and all that she had ever known. It was not a perfect place, but it was home. Andrea recalled her mother's last words to her, "Your father is a good man, Andrea. He will take care of you. You are Spanish now." And, according to the paper in her hand, she was.

Itzel had written to Ademar, and asked him to send for Andrea. He had done that, and more. King Felipe had granted her legitimacy and acknowledgment as the only daughter of Don Ademar de Piña. She was officially Spanish. It no longer mattered that she had grown up in a shop, or that her mother was brown. Itzel had told her that her whiteness came from being born under the light of the moon. It was lucky, and her life would be different because of it. She had been welcomed by the Maya people because of their love for her mother. Once Itzel died, however, Andrea no longer received the same warm welcome. She was too white to be Mayan, and before she received her certificate of legitimization from the king, too brown to be Spanish. In New Spain, with a dead Mayan mother and an absent

Spanish father, she belonged nowhere, really. There was nothing left for her, so why not go to the one person who may want her?

But how could Itzel know anything about Ademar's feelings? He had left New Spain before she was born, and it had been almost twenty years since his affair with Itzel. This was a catastrophic mistake, but Andrea had no other choice. She answered Ademar's summons and hoped she would find a father when she arrived.

# Three

*"...for hope is always born at the same time as love..."* -
Miguel de Cervantes, *Don Quixote*

Andrea straightened the narrow sleeves of her dress, unable
to stop fidgeting. She stood port side, watching the other passengers disembark. They had docked an hour earlier but had only
been allowed to leave the ship after King Felipe's port authori-
ties from the *Casa de Contratación* searched the ship's cargo, sep-
arating the passengers' luggage from the property of the king.
The *Casa* clerks scribbled in bound notebooks, counting every
tobacco leaf and grain of sugar. They ensured the king received
his tax, the cost of traveling with the protected fleet. Seag-
ulls squawked, flying in circles overhead, searching for dropped
breadcrumbs, or if they were lucky, unattended fish. She inhaled,
taking a deep breath to steady her nerves, and gazed once more
out at the sea of people at the port of Sevilla. She had no idea
who to look for. She had never met her father, for she was sure
he would meet her. Surely he would not send a servant to collect

her. Andrea grasped her bag tighter so no one could see how her hands shook.

It was now or never. The sailors glanced at her curiously, waiting for her to disembark as they finished their tasks. She resisted the urge to wipe her palms on her skirts as she clung to the small brown leather bag that contained all her belongings. Already she was set apart from the other people. She had no chaperone or servant, no trunks filled with the latest fashions; just a simple bag that carried her whole life. The leather cracked and had spots of discoloration from where saltwater had splattered it.

Courage Andrea, she whispered.

She had said her goodbyes to her old life when she left Mérida, and she could not turn coward now. She lifted her head high, shifting her grip on her bag, and placed one hand on the rope rail. It was twisted and rough, pieces of hemp breaking off in her palm, but it steadied her. Her mother had loved and trusted Ademar, and Andrea loved and trusted her mother. So with one step, and then another, she walked down the wooden ramp from the ship to the dock, carefully stepping between the raised wooden bars. All around her people greeted each other, mostly in Spanish although she did catch snippets of other languages she did not recognize, servants organizing luggage in neat piles, and the general bustle of a port. Andrea walked out of the way of those crowding the gangplank of the galleon until she reached a spot slightly out of the way.

She stood still trying to appear confident and nonchalant. Her thoughts whirled with a constant stream of, 'You belong here. You belong here.' She wondered how she could look for whoever was supposed to meet her without seeming like she was lost or without leaving with the wrong person. It struck her, not for the first time, that perhaps she had been very foolish coming here alone. But she hadn't had the heart to convince her maid Colel to leave her family for a kingdom that would not welcome her.

She spotted movement out of the corner of her eye. An elderly man, so hunched over with age that his long white beard almost touched the ground, hobbled toward her pushing a cart filled with brightly colored cloths and a jumble of trinkets. "Jewels of the New World!" he shouted, peddling his wares to anyone who would listen. He spotted Andrea looking curiously at him, and he leered at her, revealing three missing teeth. "*Señorita*, can I interest you in some nice cotton cloth? Or perhaps this silver bracelet?" The man rummaged through his cart, showing off this and that.

"It's all very lovely, but no thank you. I am waiting for someone." She tried moving away, but he followed her.

The man tried again. "What about this, señorita? This necklace came directly from a place called Santo Domingo in the name of God and King."

The crowd pushed her closer to the cart, pressing her hips uncomfortably into the side. The port was teeming with people and activity. Andrea shrank, her shoulders slumping as tried and failed not to be jostled by stray elbows and bags. She could smell the man's breath now as he stepped even closer to her. His broken fingernails caught the sunlight as he reached for a lock of her hair that had fallen over her shoulder. She shuddered backward and bumped into something firm.

"Oh, I do beg your pardon, *señor!*" She exclaimed, horrified to realize she had collided with a man.

He was obviously important, dressed in fine clothes tailored to perfection. His dark eyes glinted as he grabbed her by the shoulders to steady her. He looked her up and down before speaking sharply to the peddler who had made her so uncomfortable.

"Thank you," she said softly.

Reminded that he still had his hands on her, the man quickly released her and stepped back. "*Señorita*," he bowed slightly before straightening.

He looked at her again with his sharp eyes that took in her disheveled hair, dusty hem, and nervous wrinkling of her dress at a glance. "Do you need assistance?"

Unaccountably relieved, Andrea nodded. "I am supposed to meet my father, but," she shrugged. She could hardly admit that she had never met the man before or that she hadn't the faintest idea what he looked like to a perfect stranger, no matter how handsome he was.

Gabriel could not believe the dainty creature he had crashed into was Don Ademar's daughter, but it began to look that way. Her eyes were the same striking green as Ademar's, but that did not necessarily mean she was his daughter.

"Perhaps I may be of assistance," he offered.

She brightened. "That would be very kind of you. My father sent for me, and I have only just arrived." She smiled up at him. "It is so nice to be on solid ground again."

"What was the name of your ship, *señorita*?"

"The *San Martin*."

If only all of Gabriel's assignments were so easy!

"Is your father Don Ademar Reynaldo de Piña?" he asked, hardly daring to believe his luck.

"Yes! Do you know him *señor*?

He laughed at her bright-eyed enthusiasm. "Yes, child, I do. In fact, I was sent here to collect you."

His frowned as her smile dimmed. She expected her father to meet her, and he almost felt sorry for her that she was disappointed. Still, he reasoned, better disappointed now before she met the man than to have her hopes dashed later.

"Oh of course," she attempted a smile again. "I am Andrea."

As she curtseyed, Andrea bent her head, finally breaking contact with the man's eyes. They were so dark as to be almost black. The color was no different than those of the Maya back home, but his stared through her, making her feel that he could see all her thoughts and secrets. His clothing and bearing were not like a servant's, but why would her father send someone in his place? After all the trouble and expense of sending for her, why did he not come for her himself?

Cutting off her thoughts, the dark-haired stranger bent low before her. "Doña Andrea, I am Gabriel, the Marqués de Silva." He motioned to the side, and a servant she had not noticed leaped forward to grab her bag.

"Where is your other baggage?" Gabriel looked around questioningly. "Is it with your servant somewhere?" he asked.

"Oh," Andrea looked down at the bag she was still holding. It was battered and frayed at the opening. "This is all I have. I have no servant."

She winced, the color rising in her cheeks. She prayed things were not already ruined. She should have thought of her reputation and begged Colel to come with her. No matter that Ademar had only reserved one fare, young ladies of her new station did not travel alone.

"Have I ruined things beyond repair?" she asked quietly.

Gabriel recovered from his momentary shock. Little surprised him, but the thought of a defenseless girl sailing across the world by herself certainly fit the bill. That, and she could survive with so little clothing. He thought ruefully of his mother, who insisted on filling a separate carriage with trunks of clothing every time she undertook a journey.

He smiled gently down at Andrea, the acting coming to him more easily than he would have supposed.

"Never mind any of that," he said. "We'll keep the carriage's curtains open, and your father's housekeeper will assign a maid to you.

He offered her his arm, and they walked down the pier. It was a different experience walking with Gabriel. People jostling did not touch her, giving them a wide berth, encouraged no doubt by the stare Gabriel would give to the more boisterous fellows.

"Fashions change frequently now that King Felipe moved Court to Madrid. You were quite right to bring only a few dresses with you. Even the newest dresses would be out of fashion by the time you arrived in Sevilla. As your mother is not with you, I am certain my mother would accompany you to the modiste. Nothing would make her happier than ordering you an entirely new wardrobe."

Gabriel stunned himself with the offer. He never personally involved himself in cases, and he was especially careful to not involve his family. This case grew more unbearable by the day. His mother would like Andrea. How irritating.

# Four

*"Where one door shuts, another opens."* - *Miguel de Cervantes, Don Quixote*

The drive passed quickly, and the pier soon faded into the background. Clearly a shipping district, warehouses rose on either side of the road. Famous explorers congregated here when not sailing around the globe in search of riches for Spain. Merchants tallied their goods, overseeing industrious clerks scrambling up and down lines of containers filled with bolts of fabric or cones of sugar. A tavern on one corner overflowed with sailors, recognizable by their bowlegged gaits, walking as though they were still aboard a rolling ship.

Andrea struggled to contain her excitement at this new world so like her home, and yet so different. Already things had changed. She had never before sat in such a luxurious carriage. It was large and black, with room for four people inside to sit comfortably. A crest she assumed to be her father's proudly proclaimed its occupants as members of the de Piña family. The squabs were well-padded and lined with a soft, dense fabric.

Gabriel sat, a picture of bored elegance, legs extended with his feet crossed at the ankles.

At the sound of his stifled laugh, she reluctantly drew her face away from the window. "I suppose you have lived here a long time," she accused.

"My family has a house here," he acknowledged. "We do not spend the whole year here of course, but every man with more than a passing interest in importing goods from the New World must spend a certain amount of time at the port."

"How interesting!" Andrea exclaimed. "Do all marquesses take such an interest in trade?"

Gabriel looked interested for the first time since they entered the carriage.

"No," he admitted. "Usually the second son learns the business."

"But you are particularly enterprising?" Andrea interrupted cheekily.

She surprised a grin out of him, a sight all the more startling for how it transformed his face from a serious man to a carefree boyishness that was positively endearing.

"I like to believe so," he agreed.

"Do you have any siblings then?" she asked, wanting to learn more about the man sitting across from her who could not seem to decide whether or not he preferred to be serious or charming.

"I had a brother who died at birth." Gabriel shrugged at her little gasp of dismay. "It is quite all right, Doña. It was before I was born."

"Your poor mother," Andrea said sympathetically. "She must have been very grateful to have you."

"Maybe now," he conceded, "but I was a curious boy. I preferred taking things apart instead of putting them together."

She smiled at the vision of the curly-haired little boy she imagined him to have been. "It would have been nice to have a brother."

"Don Ademar said you have only lived in New Spain. Tell me about it?"

"It is not that interesting."

Andrea looked back out the window. The streets of Sevilla widened as they drew closer to the wealthier residential neighborhoods. Ornate columns decorated the entrances of houses, proclaiming the owner's wealth to the rest of the world. The buildings in New Spain were similar, if more colorful.

She sighed. The Marqués de Silva would never see her as his social equal if he knew about her mother. Acknowledgment as Spanish and her recent legitimization allowed her entrance into her father's world. It was the fresh start she needed.

The Marqués coughed gently, bringing her out of her thoughts. Andrea looked back at him, flushing a little. Maybe she could share a few things with him.

"I spent my whole life in Mérida. The houses look similar, but ours are painted bright colors. We lived in a blue house, the color of the sea, but there were pink houses and green, and every bright color you can think of. The streets are like rainbows." Her eyes caught his. "It is girlish and fanciful, I know, but I already miss the colors."

Gabriel was charmed despite himself.

* * *

Andrea straightened as the carriage slowed to a stop, and the door opened to reveal a grand house in the middle of Sevilla. It was two stories, with balconied windows facing the street. Columns decorated either side of the door, which was decorated with carved swirls and scrolls. Vines crawled up the walls, mingling with the balconies, and peeking into windows. The stucco gleamed white, contrasting with the dark uniforms of the servants lining up outside to welcome her. Her eyes, however, were immediately drawn to the Piña family crest above the doorway, matching the one on the carriage door. This time she looked at it more closely. Chiseled in stone were two crowned lions, fiercely guarding a knight's shield. Gabriel stepped down from the carriage first, before reaching back an arm to hand Andrea down. He noticed her eyes focused above the door.

"Do you see the tree within the shield?" Gabriel pointed. Andrea nodded. "That is the de Piña family crest. Your family crest."

She looked at the number of servants waiting to greet her and knew she would not forget how much her life had changed by becoming a de Piña. They approached a tall, dour man. His stern face softened as she walked closer.

He bowed, murmuring "Don Gabriel. Doña Andrea, welcome home."

"The butler, Francisco. Anything you need, he will get for you."

Andrea nodded. "Pleased to meet you, Francisco."

She started to curtsey out of habit but stopped at the consternation appearing in Francisco's widened eyes. A quick look at Gabriel showed him straightening the ruffles at the ends of his sleeves. Luckily he did not seem to have noticed her blunder.

"Where is Don Ademar?" Gabriel asked, taking her mind off her embarrassment, surprised the man was not waiting outside to see his daughter.

Francisco paused before leading them up the steps into the house. "I believe the marqués is in the courtyard," he said carefully. "Shall I have refreshments brought there?"

"Yes, thank you," Gabriel said.

Gabriel ushered Andrea inside the house, revealing a long hallway framed with paintings, that opened up to a small courtyard filled with trees and a bubbling fountain that was surrounded by the rest of the house. A small magpie bathed in the fountain, gargling and shaking water over its multicolored wings. The jewel tones sparkled in the sun, like the blue waters of the ocean. A set of matching metal chairs painted white nestled in the corner near a small table with a mosaic tile top. Andrea smiled at the sunshine pouring into the courtyard, knowing this would quickly become her favorite place in the house. Excitedly, she turned to Gabriel, who was watching her enthusiasm with a soft smile.

"Do you like it?" he asked her.

"I love it," she beamed, lifting her face to the sunlight. She closed her eyes, savoring the warmth and the light on her skin.

"Good."

At that, a man who been reading the newspaper folded it carefully, set it down, and stood up from the stone bench tucked away in the corner of the courtyard. He was thin, with narrow hips, and of middling height. Andrea saw few signs of aging apart from the streaks of silver at his temples, but what caught her attention were his eyes. They were bright green, a hue she had only ever seen before in a mirror.

He dressed to show his wealth, wearing a black velvet doublet intricately embroidered with silk threads and hose. Jewels glinted from his fingers as he folded his hands in front of himself. Andrea had never known a man to be so fashionable, even among the wealthiest families in New Spain. She could not help but look between him and Gabriel, comparing the two men, ultimately preferring Gabriel's simple, unadorned clothing.

"This must be my daughter," the man – her father – spoke to Gabriel after a dismissive glance in Andrea's direction.

"Yes – "

"I am Andrea," she interrupted. She stepped forward before thinking better of it and dropped a belated curtsey.

"You look so like your mother," Ademar said, sounding thoughtful.

Andrea struggled to hide her surprise. Her place in New Spain had been precarious for the very simple fact that she looked nothing like the Mayan mother who raised her. They shared a similar outspokenness and hair that was unable to hold a curl, but Andrea looked every inch a Spaniard. Perhaps Itzel and Ademar shared a closer relationship than she assumed.

She impulsively extended her hand. Ademar looked at it before gingerly clasping her hand. His grasp was light, his hand cool. Dropping his arm back to his side, Ademar turned to Gabriel, ignoring Andrea completely.

"Were you able to make contact with Marco Sandobal?" he asked.

Andrea stood still, missing Gabriel's response. Ademar clasped Gabriel on the shoulder, clearly pleased. She watched the two men numbly, a buzz in her ears. This must be shock, she thought dimly. She might not have anticipated instant kinship, but she had not expected this dismissal.

Gabriel knew the instant Andrea realized her father did not care about her presence. He had seen men react less to wounds received in battle. He watched the emotions flit across her expressive face in rapt succession. The first shock, then hurt, and finally a dull resignation. He could not fault her for hoping for a warmer reception. She stood there, motionless, looking at nothing. For a moment, he was tempted to pull her into his arms and comfort her. Luckily, he was not a man given to act upon his first impulse. The girl's father was speaking to him for heaven's sake! With a mental shake, Gabriel pulled his thoughts away from the girl and forced them back to the mission at hand. It would not do to be distracted by a pretty girl who just now seemed desperately alone.

# Five

*"Destiny guides our fortunes more favorably than we could have expected." - Miguel de Cervantes, Don Quixote*

The maid threw open the curtains, letting in the sunlight. After a few moments, the maid had prodded the fire, its warming blaze welcome in the chilled air of the morning. Andrea came awake slowly, blinking her eyes at the presence of another person in her room.

"Oh good morning, Doña. I did not mean to wake you," the girl apologized.

Andrea sat up, rubbing her eyes. "That is quite all right. I am not used to sleeping so late!"

The maid nodded and pointed to a tray sitting on a small side table near the fire. "I have a few things for you to break your fast, if you wish, Doña."

Andrea's eyes lit up at the sight of a steaming cup of coffee. With a little squeak of delight, she pulled on a dressing gown the maid handed her and sat down before the fire. She added a dollop of sugar, took a long sip, and sighed with pleasure.

"How nice it is to have coffee again."

The *San Martin* had run out of coffee halfway through the journey from the New World to Spain, and she relished the bitter taste. The smell brought back memories of afternoons in the sun, walking through the plaza in Mérida. Wealthy Spaniards would sit in cafes under the stuccoed archways, sipping on small cups of coffee gossiping and people watching. She normally drank her coffee in one gulp before hurrying downstairs to prepare for customers. She was now one of those Spaniards, savoring each sip and drinking from fine porcelain.

She looked at the assortment of pastries and jam on the tray, and carefully selected one. What a luxury to eat in her own room, to have her own room! She ate two pastries in quick succession before she felt awake. Looking at the maid, who was now making up the bed, she asked, "What is your name?"

"María, Doña."

"It is a pleasure to meet you, María. My name is Andrea."

María smiled a little before finishing with the bed. "I am to be your ladies' maid, Doña Andrea, unless you wish to hire someone new."

"I think we shall deal well together, María. You see, I have never had my own ladies' maid before. My mother and I had one maid for all the housework," Andrea frowned. "I shall rely upon you to make sure I do not look foolish."

María looked into the wardrobe and pursed her lips. "Begging your pardon, Doña, but none of these are suitable."

Andrea chuckled at the maid's obvious disapproval. Yet another thing lacking. She had not spoken with Ademar after that first day in Sevilla, and nothing had been said about a new wardrobe. If only the Marqués de Silva visited again. She had not seen him either, though she knew he worked with her father. At least he had spoken to her and listened to her. The servants she had met around the house hovered at the edges of rooms, leaving her to her own devices, and her father was just as absent as he had been while living an ocean away.

"Then I suppose we shall have to make do for now," Andrea said briskly. "Just choose what you think is best."

With a noise that clearly said no option was best, María selected a blue gown. She helped Andrea step into the dress, tightly lacing a corset over the chemise before lacing up the back. The high necked gown looked well on her, if out of date. María then gestured for Andrea to sit down to dress her hair.

"Your hair is quite nice, Doña. It is so thick," María commented as she brushed the long strands.

Andrea thanked her, marveling at the coils and twists María managed. "I knew we would deal well together," she laughed. "I can never seem to manage my hair on my own."

María blushed at the compliment. "If that is all?" she asked.

With a last admiring glance in the mirror, Andrea nodded. "Yes, thank you María. You may return to your other duties."

María bobbed a curtsey, then left the bedchamber.

Footmen and maids scurried about, attending to their responsibilities as Andrea wandered down the hallway to the main rooms of the house on the ground floor. As she walked past, peeking into this room and that, they bowed or murmured polite, if distant greetings before leaving her again in silence. Life in Spain was not so different after all. Her home may have more people living there, but she was just as alone.

Francisco eventually took pity on her and showed her to the library. "Perhaps something here may be of interest, Doña," he suggested with a sympathetic smile.

She thanked him and turned to wander the shelves as he shut the door behind him. Ademar must be wealthy indeed, to own so many books, she thought as she trailed a finger over the bindings. She had never seen so many books in one place. The thought made her a bit giddy. She had been taught to read and write, but she never had the opportunity to sit and read for plea-sure. Even if, she grimaced, there did not seem to be any novels.

Wandering over to another bookshelf, Andrea pulled down a book on Spanish history. It would be beneficial to learn about her new home, and with that happy thought, moved toward a cozy-looking nook in the corner to settle in with her book.

A creaky floorboard interrupted her.

"Oh, I am sorry for disturbing you."

It was Gabriel, as if summoned by her thoughts. He stopped abruptly in front of her settee, clutching a number of papers in his arms. A flash of emotion rippled across his face before his lips flattened. Andrea looked at him curiously. Days had passed since she had seen Gabriel last, though she knew he and Ademar shut themselves in her father's study for hours at a time.

"I did not expect to see you here."

"I needed to consult with some books about some questions your father had," Gabriel said. "Why are you not out shopping or whatever it is women do during the day?"

Andrea snorted, amused despite his disapproving tone. "I cannot buy dresses without money," she said lightly.

Gabriel's eyes narrowed, taking a closer look at her dress. She resisted – not well – the urge to squirm. She brought her book up to her chest protectively. His sharp eyes appeared to notice the hastily altered neckline and lace at the edges of her sleeves added in an attempt to make the old gown a bit more fashionable.

Had Ademar not even provided his daughter with new gowns? Gabriel had not seen the man or his daughter at any of society's events in the past week, but he had assumed Ademar had planned some grand unveiling to show off his heir. By the looks of it, Andrea was wearing the dress she had worn when he first saw her at the port of Sevilla. It had been altered slightly but was clearly the same dress. He could admit, if only to himself, that she wore the dress well, but it would not do for a marqués' daughter.

"You should tell Ademar to give you a larger allowance," Gabriel said.

"I would have to find him first. I have seen my father as much as I have seen you, which is to say, not at all," she admitted.

Gabriel had been looking for anything unusual that morning and thought he may find something hidden in between books. He had found nothing about smuggling in Ademar's study, so he had started expanding his search to other rooms in the house, beginning with the library. After collecting anything with potential, he was eager to read through the documents, but Andrea's dress had caught his notice. Why would Ademar send for his daughter only to ignore her and effectively keep her secluded?

Making a quick decision, he spoke before he could change his mind. "May I call upon you tomorrow morning?"

"Yes." She drew out the word slowly.

"Excellent. Until then." He bowed, and still holding his papers, walked out the door. Andrea stared at him, wide-eyed and feeling like she had missed an important piece of the conversation.

# Six

*"To surrender dreams – this may be madness."* - Miguel de
Cervantes, *Don Quixote*

Andrea examined her reflection critically. María had done
her best, but it was not like she had a wide range of options to
choose from. Still, she thought, her hair looked nice. Her dress
might be fraying at the hem and faded, but it fit her figure nicely.

"You are the only one who has ever managed to put my hair
up and keep it there," she told María, twisting this way and that
to glimpse the back of her head. "It always falls out of its pins for
me."

María said nothing, but a small flush gave away her pleasure
at the compliment.

"You are so lucky the Marqués de Silva is calling on you,
Señorita," she said. She clutched Andrea's nightdress, wrinkling
it in her hands as she sighed dreamily.

"Is he very popular then?" Andrea asked.

"Oh yes. And so handsome, too!" María bustled about the

room, putting the nightdress away in a drawer. "Perhaps he has taken a liking to you?" she asked slyly.

It was Andrea's turn to blush.

"Oh he couldn't possibly," she said, flustered. "The Marqués is an associate of my father's. I'm sure he is merely being kind."

María pursed her lips in obvious disagreement.

"It will be nice to have a caller though."

The maid softened with sympathy. Her young mistress' loneliness was plain to see. If only the master would take an interest in his daughter, the poor dear would be much happier. She had high hopes for the morning.

* * *

"Are you planning to tell me what is going on in that mind of yours, Gabriel?"

"No," he said simply.

The Marquesa de Silva was a beautiful, glamorous woman quite popular within Spanish society. She was intelligent and ruthless, having raised Gabriel on her own after his father died. It was from his mother, that Gabriel had learned to navigate difficult situations with diplomacy and no small amount of subterfuge. After all, Daniela managed to retain the admiration of her suitors despite rejecting every single one. Gabriel was not bringing his mother to call upon Andrea de Piña for these reasons though. His mother would be able to outfit Andrea with a new wardrobe that would allow the girl to move about in society. Her approval would also reach Ademar's ears, leading to rumors that just might loosen his tongue. Gabriel would finally be able to lay Ademar's smuggling ring to rest.

"Very well." Daniela patted him gently on the cheek. "I will go along with this scheme of yours, but only because I know you will be home to have dinner with me tomorrow night," she said sweetly, as though she had not just consigned him to hours of sitting through his mother's attempts at matchmaking.

He groaned. "Who is to be there this time?"

She smiled serenely. "If I told you, you would not attend. This way you may pretend it will just be you and I."

The carriage slowed to a stop as he grumbled, though he tried to keep it under his breath. His mother, after all, was about to do him a favor.

The house door opened and Francisco stood waiting to welcome them. Gabriel twisted the handle to leave the carriage and then held his hand out for his mother. She grabbed his hand and stepped out gracefully.

"Mamá, be nice," he reminded her.

"I will, dearest." She walked up the steps.

Francisco bowed deeply. "Welcome, Marquesa de Silva. Marqués de Silva."

The butler motioned and a footman stepped forward to take their cloaks. "Doña Andrea is in the parlor."

"Thank you, Francisco. I know the way." Gabriel inclined his head.

He turned to the right to lead his mother down the hallway to the parlor. As he pushed open the door, he suddenly felt unaccountably nervous. He surreptitiously wiped his palms on his hose cursing himself for acting like a boy. This was an assignment, nothing more.

The parlor was not the most welcoming room though, like the rest of the house, it was richly furnished. The room looked sterile, as though no one had ever sat in it before. Now Gabriel thought about it, that was likely the case. Ademar always welcomed guests into his study, and to Gabriel's knowledge, had never before had a mistress to host gatherings elsewhere in the house. His mother swept into the room, prompting Andrea to rise from a chair near a crackling fire.

"Doña Andrea, may I present my mother Daniela, the Marquesa de Silva?"

Andrea sank into a curtsey. Did he bring his mother to call upon her?

"Marquesa, Marqués. Would you like to sit? Refreshments will be here soon if you would care for some tea."

"Doña Andrea – " his mother began with a side glance at Gabriel. "I understand you have not been in Spain long."

Andrea looked at the Marquesa for some hidden meaning but saw only kindness in her eyes. They were the same color as Gabriel's, a dark brown that looked chocolatey in the firelight.

"Yes, I have only just arrived from Mérida, in New Spain."

Gabriel's mind wandered as the women spoke, his mother talking about her favorites places to visit in Sevilla (the modiste, the theater, and the park – in that order), but something Andrea said caught his attention.

"What did you say?" he demanded.

Both Andrea and Daniela looked at him, Daniela more sharply than Andrea, who merely looked taken aback.

"I often spent time down in the cargo hold on the ship," Andrea repeated, her voice lifting at the end like a question. "There was nothing improper in it," she added quickly, no doubt think Gabriel's mind had leaped to a conclusion. "There was not very much to do, and one can only stare at the sea so often."

She had no way of knowing he was concluding that she may become useful in his investigations. Andrea had seen her father's cargo during the journey and may have seen or heard something that could point Gabriel in the right direction.

"Of course you did nothing improper," he reassured her gently. "You would not wish to stay in your cabin the entire journey."

"Exactly right." Daniela joined in, seeming to understand Gabriel needed to extend the conversation in this direction.

His mother leaned forward to pick up a tart that had been delivered sometime earlier without Gabriel even noticing. "Was there much gold on board the ship, dear?" She nibbled daintily on the tart before saying innocently, "I have heard gold is everywhere in the Americas."

Lord bless his mother.

"New Spain produces more silver than gold, but yes, there were many crates filled with silver."

Daniela gestured to the silver chain she wore about her neck. "My necklace arrived on one of your father's ships. I wonder, did he bring any more back with him this time?"

"I couldn't say, Marquesa." Andrea hesitated.

"Oh please say yes," Gabriel interjected. "I am forever looking for gifts to give her when she is upset with me."

"Oh hush, I am never upset with you." Daniela smiled coyly. "I merely enjoy receiving presents."

Andrea laughed, although Gabriel looked slightly less pleased, sending an exasperated glance toward his mother.

"I am sure there was at least one necklace on board," Andrea assured the other woman. "Although, if you want to know the truth, there was less cargo than I originally thought."

"How so?" Gabriel asked, careful not to look too interested.

"When I first boarded the ship, it took two men to carry one crate, but only one man to unload it when I arrived in Sevilla." She looked puzzled.

Luckily Daniela murmured some reply because Gabriel took no more notice of the conversation.

Here was his proof. Don Ademar was not just simply bribing an official to look the other way, he was somehow changing the amount of cargo during the voyage. From here it would be a simple matter of bringing proof to the king's advisors. Perhaps he would consider a holiday after this. He was tired.

A polite cough from his mother prompted Gabriel's thoughts. He looked over at Daniela, who nodded her head significantly in Andrea's direction. Gabriel suppressed a groan. Of course, his mother thought he was pursuing the girl, never mind that she was young and unpolished. His mother spotted a pretty girl and pushed him in her direction. Daniela probably hoped Gabriel would win Andrea over before she met anyone else who could compete for her affections.

"My dear, what do you say to accompanying me to the dressmaker?" Daniela asked. Her eyes looked critically over Andrea's faded dress. "I know you are not from here, but that is no reason to be out of style."

It was a harsh, but fair assessment. "That is very kind of you,

Marquesa, but I am afraid I am unable to purchase new clothing at the present."

Daniela laughed, a sound of true pleasure. "I believe I have sufficient wealth to purchase a couple of dresses."

In the end, of course, Daniela ushered Andrea to the dress-maker, the milliner, and the cobbler. After a token number of protests, Andrea lost herself to a whirlwind of silks and lace. They began at Señora Beatriz's salon, where Andrea was quickly placed in the center of the room. Daniela dropped a word that her charge needed a completely new wardrobe, and the entire salon flurried with movement. Soft silk was draped over her, and she sighed with pleasure, barely able to resist rocking on the balls of her feet.

"Doña, please stand still!" The seamstress moaned between lips filled with pins.

Andrea grimaced and muttered an apology. Looking up, she met Daniela's laughing face.

"There is nothing like the feel of silk against skin," the Marquesa confessed. "It is impossible to remain still when you are itching to see how it looks."

Daniela was perched on a couch, sipping from a crystal glass of wine. She was beautiful, with clear, smooth skin and shining dark curls. Seamstresses bustled around her like maids, ensuring her glass remained full and offering nuts and sweets for her to nibble. The Marquesa accepted it as her due, though she knew all the girls by name.

Andrea felt a pang of envy. Standing in front of the other woman, she felt awkward and ungainly. She was much shorter than Daniela and a new dress, no matter how beautiful, would not give her the air of sophistication and glamour Gabriel's mother so effortlessly exuded.

The seamstress was pulling and draping a dark green velvet cloth around Andrea.

"There," she placed the last pin with satisfaction. "Look Doña. No gentleman can resist a Señora Beatriz creation."

Andrea hid her hands in the folds of the skirt to hide their trembling. She looked at Señora Beatriz, the owner herself, who had ventured to the front to look at Andrea's progress. The older woman smiled arrogantly, shrugging as if to say, I cannot argue with the truth.

A glance at Daniela's face said the same. She was grinning like a proud mama.

"Even my son, resistant as he is to my matchmaking efforts, will notice your beauty," she said.

"Oh? Does the marqués not wish to marry?" Andrea asked in what she hoped was a casual tone.

Daniela's growing smile showed Andrea she was not as subtle as she wished.

"Gabriel is at the age where he does not realize the benefits of a wife. Men need to have a wife before they realize they like having one."

Andrea laughed. She had never heard any woman as outspoken and confident as the Marquesa. It reminded her of her mother. Itzel had radical thoughts but only said them in the seclusion of their home. Their position in society was too precarious to be vocal. Daniela's obvious championing of Andrea gave hope things would be different here.

# Seven

*"What man can pretend to know the riddle of a woman's mind?"* - Miguel de Cervantes, Don Quixote

"Why on Earth has your father kept you away all this time, my dear girl," Doña Elena simpered. "It really is such a shame you have been kept from the right people for so long."

Andrea smiled thinly. This had been going on all afternoon, and the little patience she had left was wearing thin.

Ademar had been avoiding her. She had found an invitation next to her place at the breakfast table, and her attempts at questioning were brushed aside. Her introduction to Spanish society began with a smallish gathering of society ladies who all seemed more interested in ogling her than anything else. Andrea kept hoping Daniela would arrive, but she was well and truly alone.

She currently perched on the edge of a small couch, facing Doña Elena, who took up most of the seat. The older woman was one of the braver ones, preferring to unsettle Andrea directly rather than gossiping behind coffee cups. If she had not been the subject of such attention, Andrea would have been amused by the lack of subtlety. As it was, Andrea could not wait to return to her father's house. At least there, no one looked at her for signs of tainted blood.

"I lived with my mother until her death, Doña Elena," Andrea answered, hoping her bluntness would stop this line of questioning.

It did not.

Andrea closed her eyes and took a long drink of her coffee. It had been sweetened, but the bitter taste took her mind off the bitter words she wished she could say.

"You poor thing." Doña Elena's face rearranged into something sympathetic. "I wonder that Don Ademar is not in mourning?" The malice glittering in her eyes grew more pronounced.

Andrea flushed with anger, but another voice spoke up before she could retort.

"Jealousy does not suit you, dear Elena," an acerbic voice said.

The woman who spoke was sitting with a younger woman who looked to be her daughter. The two ladies were sitting close enough to have heard every word. Doña Elena opened her mouth to respond, but at a look from the other woman, said nothing. The daughter hid her smirk behind her hand, her eyes twinkling mischievously at Andrea.

Doña Elena stood and walked away in a huff. Andrea could not be sad to see the back of her, but she feared she had made an enemy of someone powerful. She sat more comfortably on the couch, rearranging her skirts to cover her shoes.

"You should pay her no mind."

Andrea looked up from her lap to see the young woman gracefully sit beside her. The woman looked to be around Andrea's age, and her easy smile inspired an answering one from Andrea.

"I mean it," the woman insisted. "Doña Elena is just a resentful old woman. Ignore her - I do. And if that does not work, my mother enjoys putting her in her place."

The older woman who had spoken up earlier was now in conversation with another woman. She met Andrea's gaze with a slight nod. Andrea turned back to face her companion.

"We have not been introduced. I am Andrea, *Doña* Andrea de Piña." Andrea stumbled over her new title, still not used to the honorific.

"I know who you are," the woman grinned broadly, her eyes lighting up. "All of Spain longs to meet you. I am Doña Luisa del Toro, but you shall call me Luisa and I shall call you Andrea."

Andrea passed her now empty coffee cup to a servant walking around the room. It should not surprise her that the people of Sevilla gossiped about her. It was the same in Mérida whenever someone important arrived in the city. It was almost flattering that she was now considered important enough to be the fodder for gossip. Or it would be if it did not make Andrea so nervous.

Luisa was looking at her curiously, waiting for a response.

"I did not realize my father was that important in Sevilla," she admitted.

"Oh, he is. In fact," Luisa leaned in, lowering her voice a little, "that is why Doña Elena is so upset. She made no secret that she wanted to marry Don Ademar, but he refused her, and now here you are." She leaned back and nodded matter of factly. "Doña Elena was not pleased to see a reminder of her rejection. Of course, she cannot ignore you. You outrank her. But she can be cruel."

Andrea blinked at Luisa's frankness. At least she had a better idea of what to expect now. She nodded slowly. "Thank you for telling me about Doña Elena."

"I need some excitement in my life, and I have a feeling things are about to be much more interesting with you around." Luisa grinned wickedly.

\* \* \*

Relief swept through Andrea's veins as she stepped inside the house. Armed with Luisa's promise to visit soon, she would almost feel encouraged if not for the stares still lingering on her back. Andrea collapsed onto a couch in the parlor with a sigh. Did all ladies smile to one's face and gossip behind one's back? It was all so petty. Hopefully, Luisa would not be that kind of person, for she sorely needed a friend. She groaned, rubbing her temples to erase the secret smiles and phantom whispers of *India* from women who waited to see her disgrace herself. Her mouth hurt from the efforts of keeping a polite smile on her face and ignoring the hurtful murmuring.

A maid came into the parlor, dusting cloth in hand. "Doña Andrea!" she exclaimed, her face slack with surprise. "We did not expect you home so soon."

Andrea sat up properly. "I have been gone all afternoon, Juana," she said slowly.

"Of course, Doña. I only meant, that is, your father," her voice faded. Juana clutched her rag to her chest. She glanced back through the parlor's open door nervously.

Tension prickled down Andrea's spine, her body reacting to the maid's agitation. "Is everything all right, Juana?"

Juana clutched at the cloth so tightly her knuckles showed white, twisting it in her hands, but she only nodded.

With a studied casualness, Andrea smoothed the folds of her skirts. "Will my father be joining me tonight for dinner?" she asked lightly, hopeful the change in subject would calm Juana's nerves.

It did not. Juana jolted at the mention of Don Ademar. If Andrea had not already felt suspicious, she would have certainly recognized something off in the maid's involuntary movement.

"Well?" Andrea prompted.

"I am not sure, Doña."

"Oh, well I suppose I shall ask him myself." Andrea stood as if to make her way to the door.

"No, you must not!" Juana blurted, her hand outstretched. Her cheeks flooded with the realization that she overstepped the bounds of mistress and servant.

"And why not?" Andrea demanded. After a long day in the viper's nest, her patience was nowhere to be found. She held no malice toward the innocent maid, who seemed so frightened that she could not possibly be duplicitous, but Andrea had had enough of double meanings and unspoken conversations.

"Please Doña, I am sorry, but Don Ademar is with a guest and is not to be disturbed," Juana finally admitted.

"What kind of guest?"

Juana shook her head. "I cannot say, Doña. But whenever he comes, the don is out of sorts the rest of the day."

"And so all the servants are on edge?" Andrea finished the thought aloud.

Juana nodded, once again twisting the rag vigorously.

Andrea thought for a moment. "I apologize, Juana, for causing you distress. I shall stay out of the way and allow you to return to your duties," she promised.

Juana's shoulders melted with visible relief.

Andrea left the parlor, stepping into the hallway. The door closed behind her, and she faced a decision. Turn right toward her father's study, or turn left toward the stairs the led to her bedroom on the second floor. With an embarrassingly small moment's regret for breaking her promise, Andrea turned right.

The servants were conspicuous in their absence as Andrea picked her way silently down the hall. She could hair raised voices coming from the study. She recognized one as her father's, but the second was unfamiliar. It was a deep voice, filled with anger and an edge that suggested the man was not one to be trifled with.

The heavy study door muffled the men's words, and Andrea crept closer. All but pressing her ear against the door, she still could not decipher the words, but she could tell the conversation was serious.

Andrea buzzed with curiosity. What could her father be discussing with who had the household walking on tenterhooks? And with whom? She resolved to find out.

Taking a deep breath, Andrea knocked softly before immediately opening the door to her father's study. Armed with her best smile, she prepared to plead feminine ignorance in case of disaster. She closed the door behind her to see Don Ademar engrossed in a discussion with his visitor. It was heated, and neither man noticed her walk into the room.

She waited until there was a brief lull before clearing her throat. "Excuse me, Papá," she said awkwardly. "I hope I am not interrupting?"

It was very clear that she was. The two men started and looked up at the sound of her voice. There was a pause as they looked at each other, each trying to say something with their eyes and expressions. The moment ended, and Don Ademar quickly shuffled the papers on the desk, thrusting them into a drawer before standing.

"Not at all, my dear," Ademar said belatedly. He glanced at the man sitting opposite the desk, hesitated once more as if he did not wish to introduce the man. "I would like to introduce you to Don Sebastián de Mendoza."

Don Sebastián was younger than her father, handsome in a way that seemed almost calculated. He dressed severely, but richly, in a black tunic with a shockingly white, starched ruff, and dark blue hose. His eyes were so dark as to be almost black, and they sparkled with sardonic amusement. He was frowning as Ademar introduced him, but he stood up to Andrea's hand, bowing low over it.

"And where have you been hiding this jewel, Don Ademar?" he asked, never taking his eyes off Andrea. His eyes roved over her body, and he smirked as Andrea flushed under his probing gaze.

"My daughter is lately arrived from New Spain," Ademar told

Sebastián, gesturing for the other man to sit. "Andrea, Don Sebastián is here to personally invite us to a ball he is hosting later this week."

Judging by the tension still lingering in the study, this was not at all what they had been discussing, but Andrea focused on Ademar's pleading smile. Sebastián might unnerve her, but this would be her first Spanish ball. She decided to ignore all subtext and nodded with an excitement not altogether faked.

"Thank you, Don Sebastián. This is a great honor."

Don Sebastián looked smug at her naive eagerness. "It will be the biggest event of the season," he promised.

"Indeed," Ademar agreed. "A very proper introduction to Spanish society."

They continuing discussing Don Sebastián's plans for the ball, but Andrea grew increasingly uncomfortable at his proprietary glances at her. Ademar did not seem to notice anything out of the ordinary, but during a lull in the conversation, Andrea stood, unable to sit there any longer.

"Oh no, please sit," she said as the men stood. "if you will excuse me, I have kept you from your business for too long already." Andrea dipped a light curtsey toward her father and Don Sebastián and quickly left the room.

Andrea took a deep breath as the door closed behind her, thankful to be away from Don Sebastián's roving eye. She regretted ever stepping into the study while he was there. The voice she had heard was not all like the voice he used while speaking to her, it was much angrier and authoritative. Besides, talk of a ball would never provoke such a nervous reaction from her father or the servants. They had been speaking of something much more important. She shuddered, thinking once again of Don Sebastián. He had not done or said anything inappropriate, not with her father in the room, but the way he looked at her made her skin crawl. He looked at her like she was his prey.

\* \* \*

Gabriel, Marqués de Silva, was not having a good day. His usually meticulous valet Manolo, to the man's horror, nicked his neck while trimming his beard causing him to rush through the rest of his ablutions. His mother expected him promptly at 10 o'clock, and would not hesitate to subject him to the disappointed stare he swore she practiced in a mirror for just these occasions.

Bracing himself for the inevitable onslaught of maternal meddling, he knocked on the front door of his parents' house. The house looked like all the others in the neighborhood, its stone facade forbidding. The receiving rooms also looked to intimidate, but Gabriel knew the family rooms held a lifetime of warmth and laughter.

The family's butler opened the door. His stern expression remained unchanged when he saw Gabriel at the door, but the corners of his eyes crinkled in Luis' best approximation of a smile. Gabriel resisted the urge to scratch at the itchy cut on his neck as Luis took his cloak. The older man carefully held the garment in his arms.

"The Marquesa is in the morning room, Master Gabriel," he said with the proprietary tones of an old family retainer.

"Thank you, Luis."

Gabriel strode down the wide hallway, ignoring the imposing paintings of glorious ancestors meant to intimidate guests with the de Silva's importance. He was the only son and heir of one of King Felipe's advisors; he and feelings of inadequacy were old acquaintances. He had put away childhood traumas long ago, but there were times like today when he could feel them creeping up behind him. Carefully arranging his face into a neutral expression, Gabriel twisted the burnished doorknob to open the parlor door.

His mother sat perched on a loveseat, her serene face hiding the sharply inquisitive mind that made her a force to be reckoned with. Despite the history of strong women in Spain, most nobles overlooked Daniela de Silva's cunning in favor of her pretty face and charming matters. Of course, that was just how his mother liked it.

She extended her hand toward Gabriel as he entered the parlor. He bent low over her hand, holding it gently. "Mamá."

"Sit, sit," she gestured with an elegant flick of the wrist toward the sofa facing her. "Would you like anything to drink?"

"No thank you, Mamá."

He sat, carefully arranging himself into a casual position. Gabriel loved his mother, but when she looked as carefree as she did right now, he knew he was in for it. He resisted the urge to squirm like a recalcitrant child, but Daniela's eyes twinkled, seeing through him. It was hopeless to hide anything from his mother.

She waited until he had made himself comfortable, before speaking. "Doña Andrea is a lovely girl."

"Yes, I suppose she is," Gabriel agreed.

"How old are you now, Gabriel?" she asked.

"Thirty."

"Then you must know that it is time to do your duty by your family. I will admit that you have made yourself useful, the king himself would be the first to agree, but it is time to fulfill your familial obligations."

Familial obligations? Gabriel was beginning to see what this was all about and felt a bit foolish for not expecting this talk sooner. His mother certainly did not waste any time. He was surprised he had lasted until thirty years old before his mother tried in earnest to get him to settle down. Felipe would have done well to deploy her to places of unrest. Daniela could conquer the entire world for Spain if she wished.

"I have a number of suitable prospects in mind. As a de Silva, you will, of course, look among the best families for a match," she paused at the look on her son's face.

"Gabriel, you are my only son. You must get married!" she said, her calm demeanor finally cracking at the edges.

Gabriel tried to smile at her, though it came out more as a grimace.

"I know I must get married, Mamá," he said carefully, "but I do not see a reason for such haste."

"That is because you are a man," Daniela replied primly. "I will see you married before the year is out. And that is a promise."

Something a little like fate slivered over Gabriel. At the time he shook off the feeling, only later pinpointing this moment as the moment he was plunged into something much deeper than himself and his matchmaking mama.

# Eight

*"I was born free..." - Miguel de Cervantes, Don Quixote*

Andrea breathed in to allow María to tighten her laces. A tremor shook her body, and María paused. She looked at her mistress and gingerly rested her hand on Andrea's shoulder. The slight weight was comforting, as was the concerned look on the maid's face.

"Doña?"

It had been a long time since someone had looked at her like they could see every bit of her loneliness. And it had even longer since she had felt a friendly touch. She relished the warmth spreading across her back.

"I'm all right," Andrea reassured her.

She attempted a smile, her lips faltering into a grimace. Glancing into the mirror, Andrea looked past her reflection to meet María's steady gaze. María said nothing, but her open face made Andrea want to confide in her.

"I - I am afraid," she admitted eventually, twisting her hands together.

"What if no one asks me to dance? I know the ladies are hesitant to welcome me," she began, thinking of her one previous foray into Spanish society, "but what if they all hate me?"

Andrea turned to face María. "What if coming here was a mistake? I have never been to this sort of occasion."

María reached out to firmly grab Andrea's shoulders, turning her back to face the mirror. She briskly tied the laces and held up Andrea's dress for her to step into.

"Women can be cruel to other women, Doña," she offered.

Andrea nodded, not really listening. Visions of standing alone by the wall while fashionable lords and ladies laughed at her behind their hands assailed her. Oh, why could she not stay at home?

Seeing Andrea's increasing panic, María's normally stern face softened. "Don Ademar will be with you tonight and will make sure that all goes well."

Andrea nodded, taking a deep breath. This was why she had to attend the ball. Her father was finally showing interest in her, and she could not disappoint him. She gingerly stepped into the dress, careful not to step on the delicate hem. The maroon silk rustled as Maria fastened the buttons. The cut was more daring than any Andrea had worn before, its low cut bodice brushing the top of her chemise. Andrea had balked during the fitting, but Daniela insisted it was the height of fashion. A narrow piece of lace lined the silk edge, providing extra cover, if not comfort. She hoped Daniela was right, she could not give society any extra reason to reject her.

"There," María announced, satisfied. "You are ready."

\* \* \*

Andrea was tired. She was tired of standing against the wall watching the couples dance to a string quartet. She was tired of pretending that all she knew was Spain when she so desperately missed the lush jungles surrounding Mérida with their colorful birds and spiky iguanas, and most importantly, she missed her mother who would have shared her discomfort with the overwhelming luxury of the party.

Hundreds of candles dripped wax onto the floor, while footmen wandered around the ballroom holding trays of wine. A large table in the corner was laden with small tarts and sweets, constantly replenished by even more footmen. The room itself was magnificent, large enough to comfortably fit the hundred or so guests. Even her father's house was not so opulent, Andrea mused, as she stared at the small marble figurines resting on matching pedestals in front of each column that lined the room. Swathes of rich satin were artfully draped in the few spaces where there were no candles. If her mother were here, Itzel would have stayed long enough to catalog every fashion before returning home to make plans for new imports into the shop. Of course, if Itzel were here they never would have been invited. With a sigh, Andrea accepted a glass of wine from a passing servant and sipped it gratefully, the wine relaxing the tension in her shoulders.

Her father, Don Ademar Reynaldo de Piña, met her mother during the conquest of Mexico. Itzel was a young, naive woman at the time, only seventeen years old. Andrea's mother had rarely spoken of it, but she liked to imagine Itzel grinding maize for flour, gossiping with her friends, before looking up to see Don Ademar riding into the village on a white horse. Andrea hoped there was love in her parents' relationship. She knew her mother loved Don Ademar, and her father had spoken fondly of Itzel the one time they had spoken of her past in Mérida. Don Ademar had even publicly acknowledged Andrea as his daughter and had sent Itzel an allowance in New Spain. Many others, she knew, were not so fortunate.

She did not feel so fortunate now. She was unaccustomed to mixing in such high society, though she supposed she could be included in that rarified circle now. And, as her father had told her, it was time to forget about returning to Mérida. Her mother was dead, and so was her old life. The daughter of a marqués could not own a shop that catered to the middle class. As a woman, she could own her business, but it was clear her father expected her to marry well to support his business goals, not hers. It was naive, but she had not realized that living with her father would mean that he controlled her future. He had left her to her own devices for weeks, seemingly forgetting that he even had a daughter. He gave her no *duena* and the Marquesa de Silva provided her wardrobe. For whatever reason, it seemed that tonight he wanted to play the attentive papa, and she would let him.

So there Andrea stood, almost leaning against the wall, watching the couples dance at Don Sebastián's ball, feeling like an outsider.

As the daughter of a marqués, her presence at the ball was undisputed. It helped, too, that she looked the part. Dressed in her maroon silk gown, Andrea was the epitome of the Spanish lady. The dark color emphasized the paleness of her skin, and her coiffure elongated her neck elegantly. The current dance ended, and she quickly stifled a gasp of excitement as a young caballero approached her. He bowed elaborately, creating a long line from his pointed nose to his outstretched leg.

He was dressed to attract attention, his doublet intricately embroidered with silver thread. His linen ruff had been starched so stiffly Andrea worried he may cut himself if he turned his head too quickly. Despite that, he was handsome in a fashionable way. Ademar followed closely behind him.

"There you are, Andrea," Ademar said. "May I introduce Don Alonso?"

The caballero bowed again, only slightly less formally.

"Good evening, Doña Andrea." Don Alonso straightened. "May I have this dance?"

"You may." Andrea took his proffered hand, and he lead her to the center of the room where other couples were lining up to dance.

The music began, and Andrea sank into a curtsy, barely able to contain her excitement. Her first dance in Spain! She could only be grateful that it was a dance that had made its way to Mérida as the dance began in earnest, and Don Alonso spoke.

"Are you enjoying yourself this evening, Doña Andrea?"

"Very much. It is all so elegant," she replied.

Don Alonso proved a competent dancer, light on his feet, and good enough to ignore any missteps Andrea made. He said nothing to her through the entire dance, and she was relieved when the set ended.

Don Alonso returned her to her father at the end of the dance. Ademar was speaking with the host, Don Sebastián.

"Thank you for the dance, Don Alonso," Andrea said.

"Certainly, Doña Andrea. We must dance again. Your maroon silk matches quite nicely with my fawn doublet." Don Alonso looked down at his brown doublet appraisingly before nodding in satisfaction. "Yes, we look quite well together."

She heard a snicker to her left. Don Sebastián sneered at the dandy before cutting in. "I say, there is a young lady over there whose gown looks to be of the same velvet," he said nodding across the ballroom.

Don Alonso looked interested. "Indeed? I wonder if she has a partner for the next dance..." He bowed distractedly and wandered away in search of the woman.

Ademar chuckled, "Sebastián, you dog," he ribbed good-naturedly.

Andrea smiled weakly, more to be polite than out of any actual agreement.

"Daughter, you remember your host Don Sebastián?" Ademar asked.

"Of course," she nodded. "The ball is splendid Don Sebastián. I have never seen anything quite like it," she gushed.

Sebastián looked pleased. He was younger than she had thought at first glance, the harsh planes softened by his smile. He looked about the room in satisfaction before his eyes narrowed at something behind her. Before she could say anything, he returned his attention to her.

"Doña Andrea, I simply must have this next dance." He ushered her to the dance floor without waiting for a response, although with Ademar's grin he likely thought he did not need one.

Andrea hesitated before placing her hand on Don Sebastián's outstretched arm as they moved to line up for the minuet. The dance began and she went through the motions mechanically. This dance was different from the one with Don Alonso. She was not sure why, but something about Don Sebastián unsettled her.

"Thank you for inviting me tonight," Andrea said again, to break the silence. "It is really quite lovely."

Don Sebastián bowed his head, accepting her statement as no less than his due.

After a few moments, Andrea tried again. "This is my first ball since arriving in Spain."

"Then I am honored Doña. Did you go to many parties in New Spain?"

"Some," she said slowly. "This is much more elaborate."

Don Sebastián tensed his arm, pulling her closer to him than was warranted by the dance. She swallowed uncomfortably, glancing at the other couples near them. No one seemed to notice anything untoward, so she held her tongue, hoping it was her own lack of sophistication that made her nervous.

"Has your father ever told you about his time in the New World?" Don Sebastián's eyes glinted mockingly at her, aware of her discomfort, but doing nothing to alleviate it.

"Very little."

"He does not tell you stories, or show you what he collected?"

"My father does not like to speak of the past." He does not like to speak to me at all, she thought.

Sebastián looked frustrated, moving his face closer to hers.

Andrea instinctively pulled back. His grip tightened painfully on Andrea's, twisting her fingers. "Are you in your father's confidence?" He asked with deceptive casualness, nodding to some of the other couples dancing near them.

Andrea tried to wriggle out of Don Sebastián's grip, but he held her too tightly. "No, I am not. Whatever you want, ask him."

"He knows what I want. And, ah, I want you."

He could not be serious. Men did not declare themselves to girls like her within one dance, particularly not with such a look. He seemed more likely to strangle her than to kiss her. A laugh edging on hysteria escaped her.

"Me?" Andrea gulped.

"Yes, *querida*. I find myself quite overwhelmed by your beauty." Don Sebastián was trying very hard to flirt with her, but Andrea's common sense and his continued grip on her hand told her of his insincerity.

"I hardly know what to say," Andrea demurred, looking away. In fact, she had a great many things to say, but none of them were polite, so she held her tongue.

"Say that I may call upon you tomorrow."

She wished she could say no, but he was her host, and judging by the approving looks Ademar kept bestowing upon her, a favorite of her father's. She nodded, resigned.

Not soon enough the music ended and Sebastián bowed, pressing his lips hard against her hand, before finally releasing her. He abruptly turned around and left Andrea standing there, alone on the dance floor. More than slightly disturbed. She did not like Don Sebastián, and could not like how he was pursuing her so obviously and quickly. She absently wiped the back of her hand against her skirts. More than one thing bothered her about that dance. Before she could think any more about it, her only friend in Spanish society hurried up to her.

"Andrea!" A young woman with glossy black ringlets embraced her. Luisa del Toro was beautiful and highly sought after by all the eligible, and some not so eligible, bachelors of the Spanish court. They had reconnected at the beginning of the ball but had scarcely seen each other since then as her friend had spent every single dance with a partner. Andrea was grateful to see a friendly face after her scare with Don Sebastián.

"Andrea, did you see? The Marqués de Silva is speaking with your father!" Unaware of Andrea's mood, Luisa tugged Andrea towards the side of the room, practically skipping in her excitement.

Amused, Andrea turned to face her friend. "Forgive my ignorance, Luisa, but why are you so excited about this? Surely my father may speak with whomever he likes?"

"Of course, but the Marqués is one of the handsomest and richest men in the country." Luisa swooned slightly, before recovering herself. "And," she added thoughtfully, "quite unattached. If his red coat did not clash with my dress, I would be jealous of you."

Luisa was wearing a demure pink gown, with sleeves trimmed with white lace, that showed her off to great advantage. "Oh, hush. You look lovely and you know it." Andrea said.

"Of course I know it," Luisa laughed, fluttering her fan flirtatiously. A nearby young gentleman stumbled at the sight.

Andrea and Luisa linked arms as they moved out of the ballroom to sit in a more secluded area near the refreshments. "What could they be talking about?" Andrea wondered. She had not seen the Marqués de Silva in days, though she had to admit, she had thought about him on more than occasion.

"There's only three things de Silva would be discussing with your father. Horses, business, or you," Luisa said matter of factly.

"How can you be so sure?" she laughed.

"I am an authority on these things darling. Or rather, my mother is, and I learned from the best," Luisa smirked.

Andrea looked thoughtfully over at the Marqués de Silva. Gabriel, not that she would ever call him that, looked particularly handsome that evening. He was tall, his dark hair unpowdered and cropped close to his head. He had a stern face, with a straight Aquiline nose and high cheekbones. He wore no baubles, only an emerald stick pin in the folds of his jacket. He turned his head suddenly, his eyes finding hers in the crowd. Andrea's cheeks turned pink, embarrassed to be caught staring, and she quickly ducked behind a conveniently located potted plant.

"He does not look very friendly, does he?" Luisa commented.

"Oh no, Luisa, you cannot deny he's better looking than the other men here."

Strains of a violin began playing, interrupting Luisa before she could make a comment certain to embarrass her. Distracted, Luisa looked down at her dance card.

"Don Martín," she groaned. "All he does is recite odes to my eyes."

Andrea laughed, grinning at her friend. "Play nicely Luisa. Not all men can be eloquent in the face of such beauty."

Luisa smirked, turned on her heels, and flounced away in search of the poetic Don Martín. Andrea was left on her own but did not have long to wait until she was approached by her father, the Marqués Gabriel de Silva in tow. "Andrea, are you enjoying the party?" Don Ademar asked. "I have not seen you since you danced with Don Sebastián."

"Yes, Papá. I am having a lovely time," Andrea replied, finding it difficult to meet his eyes.

"Good, good." Don Ademar gestured to the Marqués beside him. "You remember the Marqués de Silva?"

"Charmed," Gabriel drawled in the voice he reserved for society. The bored look on his face vanished as he straightened from a bow and met Andrea's gaze. His eyes quickly moved to focus on the necklace clasped around Andrea's throat. "What a unique necklace. It is quite stunning."

"Thank you, Marqués. It was a gift from my father." The necklace was a beautiful example of New World craftsmanship, with a large turquoise pendant on a delicate silver chain. The pendant lay in a silver bezel wrapped with delicately formed silver vines.

Unnoticed by either of them, Ademar slipped away, a calculating grin hovering at his lips. Gabriel moved closer to Andrea. "Your father is very generous."

"He has been kind to me." Andrea hedged. Ademar's kindness only occurred when others would be able to see the results.

"May I ask where he found your necklace? It seems like something my mother would like." Gabriel wanted to follow up with more questions, but his mind blanked at Andrea's bright green eyes and her guileless smile. This lapse in focus had never happened to him before. It was quite unsettling.

"He found the turquoise in New Spain, Marqués. He made it into a necklace for my mother, but never had the chance to give it to her, so it came to me." Andrea's face crumpled briefly with sadness before she looked up at Gabriel again. "It is a good reminder of her though," she said, gripping the pendant tightly.

Gabriel told himself sharply that agents of the king did not feel remorse, even if the eyes of their target shone with tears.

"I am so sorry, Doña Andrea. I had no idea. I did not mean for you to recall something sad." Gabriel took Andrea's hand, bending low over it. He straightened, pretending not to notice her elevated color.

The musicians taking up their violins reached his ears. "Would you like to dance?" he asked politely.

Andrea took his extended arm and they moved to the dance floor. Gabriel expertly navigated her through the swaying couples as they joined the dance already in progress. The musicians were playing a French tune, and Andrea stumbled, unfamiliar with the choreography. Looking around, she surprised a twinkle of mirth in Gabriel's eyes. Her own ready laugh sounded, and she smiled an apology.

"I'm afraid many of these dances are quite new to me. We do not have the same dances at ho- I mean, where I am from."

Oh, why did she have to mention that! He likely would have only thought her clumsy but know he would know her complete lack of sophistication. She hoped none of the listening ears around her would report her mistake to her father. At least Gabriel already knew a little of her background, but certainly, no one else needed to know. She had to remember she was a Spaniard now and nothing else.

"Then we shan't torment your poor feet any longer," he responded at once. Gabriel took her hand, gently pulling her out from the line of dancers. Andrea followed, trying to keep her skirts from being stepped on. Gabriel led her to a corner of the room that had plaster pillars surrounding the doorframe. Elegant settees and chairs were pushed up against the walls, but neither made a move to sit. Andrea looked up into his warm brown eyes that were so gentle now.

The ballroom suddenly grew stuffy. On the nearby dance floor, women were being twirled by their partners, silken skirts fluttering in time with the music. She saw Luisa whispering with Don Sebastián and absently wondered at what happened with Don Martín. Nothing could distract her from the heat in her cheeks, however, as she realized the Marqués was still holding her hand. It was shocking how different she felt at Gabriel's attentions compared to Don Sebastián's. She would wonder why if not for the glares of every matchmaking mama. They stared at her, whispering, wondering why the handsome Marqués de Silva was singling her out. Realizing that this must be improper, her hand fluttered in his, trying to escape.

Gabriel looked down at this and frowned. How long had he been holding her hand? He felt unnerved that this girl made him forget his veneer of distance. He immediately released Andrea's fine-boned hand and took a step back, hoping to recover his professionalism with a little distance.

"Would you permit that I call upon you tomorrow?" He asked formally, not looking directly at her.

"Yes," she answered.

Gabriel nodded, bowed, and walked away without another word. Andrea stood there, staring after him blankly.

Not a second later, Luisa rushed over. "What was all that about, Andrea?" She asked, breathlessly.

Andrea looked around. "What happened to Don Martín? The music is still playing Luisa," she chastised her flighty friend. Instinct told her not to mention seeing Luisa with Don Sebastián instead of her dance partner.

She hoped going on the offensive would make Luisa forget her questions, for although nothing really happened, Andrea could not ignore how quickly her heart was beating.

Predictably, this did not work. Luisa waved her hand impatiently. "This is far more important. What did he say?"

"He asked to call upon me tomorrow."

Andrea felt out of her depth at Luisa's knowing grin. She did not have much experience with men in social settings, and the Marqués Gabriel de Silva was very much a man. She was already out of sorts from her strange dance with Don Sebastián, and the attentions from the Marqués tied her stomach in knots. She wished she had just a drop of Luisa's predilection for flirtation.

Luisa noticed none of Andrea's discomfort. She simply clapped her hands, delighted. "This is the beginning of your success," she promised.

"Of course not. The Marqués is an associate of my father's. He likely only wishes to charm him into more business."

Andrea attempted a laugh, but the skeptical look on Luisa's face told her she had not succeeded at diverting her friend's attention.

# Nine

*"...you are a king by your own fireside, as much as any monarch on his throne."* - Miguel de Cervantes, Don Quixote

The day after the ball dawned brightly, yet Gabriel noticed none of the birds nor the clear blue sky. He nodded to acquaintances passed on the streets but ignored their attempts to stop for a conversation. Felipe expected him at the palace promptly at ten o'clock, and you did not keep the king waiting.

It had to be said, as much as Gabriel enjoyed the thrill of chasing after something for the glory and honor of Spain, he was looking forward to a time when he was not an agent of the Crown. Felipe obsessed over proving himself worthy of the throne, a preoccupation that began four years earlier after his coronation and extended to all who worked for him. Felipe inherited a Spain unified in name, with an ever-expanding global influence. England at times acted as a necessary ally against France, who constantly vied for European dominance, and Spain seemed to be in a constant war to protect its empire. Despite the silver arriving in greater amounts from the New World, there were never enough funds to support the wide-reaching, bureaucratic government. Felipe's father left a legacy of debt to the Spanish Crown, and Felipe was on the verge of declaring bankruptcy. Merchants cheating the *Casa de Contratación* only hurt themselves. A bankrupt kingdom could not afford the protection merchant ships needed for the journey to and from the New World.

Spain had not long been under one rule. Multiple cultures clashed at being forced together, uncomfortably rubbing elbows under a Catholic king. The Moriscos of Granada posed an ever-growing threat of civil war, requiring Felipe's constant attention and large sums of money. Now, Felipe did not always trust his advisors, preferring to deal with matters of state directly. His wife, Queen Mary of England, had died leaving a Protestant on the throne who rejected newly widowed Felipe's offer of continued alliance. With England no longer an ally, Spain needed the riches of the New World to retain her position of power. Money kept ships seaworthy and men at their posts. Felipe relied upon the royal fifth as a major source of income. Felipe also relied upon Gabriel who, unlike other agents, had proven himself to his king time and time again. He also had the power to move around society with ease. It was Gabriel's responsibility to track down missing shipments of New World silver to bolster the Crown's coffers so that Spain could continue to protect herself.

And so Gabriel presented himself at the palace at ten o'clock precisely, the Duque of Alba paced in an antechamber waiting for him. The man's worries weighed heavily on him, evidenced by the slump of his shoulders and the occasional sighs that escaped his lips. The Duque looked up as a footman announced Gabriel's arrival, and grew visibly relieved.

"Marqués!" The Duque of Alba ushered him into the small, well-appointed room. "His Majesty will be most pleased to see you. It has been a rather trying morning," he said with a slight grimace.

Gabriel understood the feeling. It was not easy working for a man who would have rather done the work himself.

He nodded acknowledgment to the king's advisor and walked through the connecting double doors into the king's study. Felipe sat in the center of the room, behind his desk. Head bent, pen scratching at the paper, there was an untouched plate of *pan dulce* near his elbow, brought in by some exasperated servant in the hopes the king would take a small break to eat. He was a handsome man, with the light eyes and pale skin so favored by the Spaniards. While he dressed simply, Felipe's desk did not reflect the same order. The large oak desk was covered in papers and maps interrupted with creases from how often they were referenced. After Gabriel stood there for an age, Felipe looked up from his notes, his blue eyes sparkling with intelligence.

"Your Majesty," Gabriel bowed deeply.

"Sit, Marqués." Felipe gestured to a straight-backed chair facing the desk. It was austere, the lack of padding intentional. "We presume you know why we have called you here."

Gabriel shook his head, smothering a smile. Felipe always asked this question, knowing that Gabriel would never presume to know the answer.

"It has come to our attention that," Felipe checked a paper in front of him, "Don Ademar Reynaldo de Piña has not submitted the royal fifth from his most recent imports from New Spain."

Gabriel was unsurprised. Of course, the king would check on his progress before he had any tangible evidence of where Ademar hid the cargo reserved for taxes. Before he could speak up to share what he had learned, however, the king continued.

"Don Ademar's daughter has recently arrived in Spain, and now stays at her father's house in *el centro*."

"Don Ademar's daughter?"

This time Gabriel was surprised. He knew why he was trying to not be interested in Andrea, but could not think why the king would mention her. To be sure, it had caused quite a stir when Ademar announced first the existence of a daughter and subsequently her arrival in Spain, but what did she really have to do with anything? Gabriel had tried to question her as unobtrusively as possible, and whatever she knew, she was clearly unaware of it. He struggled to refocus on the king.

"Yes," Felipe continued. "Informants tell me she may have brought the royal fifth with her, or even concealed it for Don Ademar. If she has it, we want you to find it."

"Of course, Your Majesty. But," Gabriel hesitated, "what if she does not have the royal fifth? I have spoken with her, and she does not seem to have any knowledge of its existence."

The king's eyes narrowed in defense at Gabriel's protestation, before turning coy. "Doña Andrea de Piña is young and said to be quite beautiful..." His voice trailed off for a moment.

"If you pursue her, you will be able to search the house more freely than you can now as Don Ademar's associate. The Crown needs these resources. You must do your duty as a Spaniard."

Gabriel swallowed nervously. He was not looking for an attachment, and definitely did not want to encourage his mother's machinations, but he could not deny being intrigued by Doña Andrea de Piña. He would do what he must for the king, and be glad it provided him with an opportunity to discover why she fascinated him so much. She was an unknown quantity, that was all. He would get to know her, and then her allure would fade with knowledge, it always did.

"I will find what you are owed, Your Majesty. If the girl knows anything, you may be sure she will tell me."

# Ten

*"...it is the part of wise men to preserve themselves to-day for to-morrow," - Miguel de Cervantes, Don Quixote*

"Oh, you must buy these gloves, Andrea! They're positively divine."

Luisa shoved a pair of admittedly fine gloves into her hands. The soft, buttery leather glided over her skin as Andrea inspected the stitching at the fingertips. It was solid craftsmanship, as was everything on display in the shop Luisa dragged her to that morning.

"They are very nice, Luisa," Andrea agreed, "but I do not need a new pair."

She set the gloves back on the display counter and smiled apologetically at the shopgirl. "I will be sure to remember these when I need some."

The girl nodded, and the flash of disappointment on her face quickly faded as she turned toward Luisa, whose maid staggered under the bundles of hats and scarves and who knew what else. Clearly, Luisa would be making the bulk of the purchases today.

"Has no one ever told you that you do not shop for things you need, but rather for things you want?" Luisa asked, still looking at gloves, although now choosing between a brown or gray pair.

Andrea bristled at her patronizing tone. Luisa didn't mean anything by it, of course. She spent money without knowing its value because she could and she always had. Ademar had a line of credit at all the shops, so Andrea supposed she, too, could spend money with impunity, but old habits died hard. She still felt like that shopgirl who had enough money for the things she needed, but with little left over for anything frivolous. She certainly did not like spending money that was not hers, that she had not earned.

In the end, Andrea selected a violet ribbon. She knew what it meant to the shopgirl, and she did have money now, albeit her father's, even if she would never be able to bring herself to just buy anything she wanted. The girl wrapped the ribbon in a small bag, handing it to Andrea with a soft thank you.

Luisa plucked the bag out of Andrea's hands, handing it to María, who was accompanying her. María walked behind the ladies with Luisa's maid. They chatted quietly, with an ease born of mutual position and acquaintance. Luisa, meanwhile, was chattering enough for the two of them, requiring nothing more from Andrea besides the occasional nod or murmured agreement.

The sun beamed down at them, or it would have been if Luisa closed her parasol. Even here with a weaker sun, they were expected to protect their pale skin. Nevertheless, Andrea enjoyed the sunlight reflecting off the light stone walls. The port was too far away to see, but she could taste the salt in the air and that was enough.

"...don't you agree?"

Andrea looked blankly into Luisa's expectant face, which clearly expected a response. Before Andrea could ask her to repeat herself, a deeper voice hailed them. Don Sebastián sauntered down the street toward them, his hat tipped at a rakish angle.

"Doña Luisa, Doña Andrea," he dipped his head at them.

"Don Sebastián," Luisa dropped into a graceful, if too deep, curtsey.

Andrea quickly followed suit.

"And what have you ladies been up to today?" he asked with a pointed glance at the parcels behind them.

"Just a bit of shopping. Surely you would not have me in an out of fashion dress?" Luisa fluttered her eyelashes flirtatiously.

Sebastián brought his hand up to his chest. "Never, my lady," he said with mock horror.

"And you, Doña Andrea? What did you purchase?"

"Oh, just a ribbon for my hair." Andrea tucked a piece of hair that was falling out of her bun behind her ear self-consciously.

"Only one ribbon? Surely Don Ademar can spare some pesos for a new dress after his latest shipment in from the New World."

Andrea missed how his eyes sharpened despite his teasing words. As it was, Andrea noticed nothing amiss, thankful for Luisa's skill in flirtation as she once again captured Don Sebastián's attention.

\* \* \*

The front door swung open as Gabriel walked up to the de Piña residence.

"Good afternoon Marqués de Silva." Francisco bowed deeply before standing aside to allow Gabriel inside.

"Good afternoon, Francisco. Is Doña Andrea in?" he asked as the butler took his coat and hat.

"She is in the courtyard, Marqués."

"Excellent." Francisco turned to summon a footman to escort him, but Gabriel interjected, "No, no. I know the way." He grinned his thanks at the man before walking down the corridor toward the door that opened out into the courtyard.

Andrea had not yet noticed his presence, and he took a moment just to observe her. She was engrossed in a book, squinting every so often when the sun provided too much glare on the page. The sun glinted off her dark hair, deepening its black color. She let out a quiet laugh as something in the story must have amused her. He took that moment to speak.

He cleared his throat. "Good afternoon, Doña Andrea."

Several things happened at once. Andrea dropped the book in surprise and it fell crumpled first into her lap then onto the floor as her chair squeaked, scraping across the ground, and Gabriel lost his battle to keep a straight face. His laughter rang out, so infectious that Andrea's irate glare gradually melted into amused resignation and she let out a reluctant chuckle.

"If you are quite finished," she said with pretend hauteur, "may I offer some refreshment?" She gestured for him to sit as she picked up her book, smoothing out the pages, and resettled herself in her chair.

"Yes, thank you." He debated mentioning the Incident, as he would forever think of it, before noticing Andrea's elevated color. Sensing she was not as composed as she seemed, he changed the subject.

"My mother sends her regards. You were a grand success at Don Sebastián's ball, and she is taking the credit for it to anyone who will listen."

"As she should! It was all thanks to her impeccable taste in gowns," Andrea responded, pleased.

"Well, please do not tell her that when you next see her. She does not need the encouragement," Gabriel groaned good-naturedly.

Andrea reached out to give him a playful swat on the arm. His breath caught, but luckily she did not seem to notice. Or perhaps she did, for she immediately rose and went to the door. She peeked her head through the doorway and said something to the footman who promptly bowed his head and took off down the hallway.

She turned back toward him, a gentle smile on her face. "I asked them to send something up from the kitchen."

"Excellent, I find myself quite hungry all of a sudden," he said, patting his flat middle.

The footman returned to the courtyard sooner than Gabriel expected, carrying a tray with some watered down wine along with a snack of freshly baked bread and cheese. He found himself actually growing hungry as his mouth watered at the smell of the still-warm bread. Andrea quickly poured two glasses and handed him one.

"You visit my father often, Marqués," Andrea noted after he had taken a sip.

"I do," he agreed. "I have lately been assisting Don Ademar with his business."

He reached for some bread, tearing a small chunk from the loaf. A small waft of steam rose, attesting to its freshness.

"What do you do when you are not helping my father?"

Gabriel almost smiled at her frankness. Most young ladies of Andrea's position cared more for the money that trade routes provided them than the business itself. But he was quickly learning that Andrea was no ordinary noblewoman.

He thought for a moment at how to answer her question. He could not tell her the whole truth, of course, but he could tell her something. Some honesty may even help him in his investigation. It was worth the gamble, so he decided to tell her a version of the truth.

"I assist the Crown from time to time."

"The Crown?" Her mouth dropped open.

"Yes, the Duque of Alba mostly along with a few others."

"A few others, like the King?" She looked impressed.

Gabriel nodded. He crossed his legs, trying to get more comfortable in a chair that suddenly felt too small for his rapidly inflating ego.

"Are you able to tell me what you do for the king?" she pressed.

"I can tell you some." His voice lowered, and he leaned forward with great drama.

Andrea leaned forward, mirroring his actions.

"I am looking into some smuggling," he hedged, knowing that he needed to capture her interest, not her suspicion.

"Smuggling? How intriguing." Andrea nibbled thoughtfully on a piece of cheese. "Yes, I can see how Papá would be helpful."

Gabriel had been distracted by the movement of her lips, but at this, he snapped to attention. "Why do you say that?" he asked, tightly.

"Well," she said, looking at him curiously, "my father works along the same trade routes. Surely he would have some knowledge of smuggling. Isn't that why you are helping him?"

Somehow Andrea had gotten – mostly – to the heart of the matter without realizing he was actually investigating Ademar. He just needed to play the rest of this conversation carefully so she did not realize the whole of it.

"Yes, you have found me out, I'm afraid." He leaned back in his chair and gave Andrea his best grin. "How very smart you are," he added, teasingly.

Andrea giggled nervously at his flirting, quite unlike her usual outrage when a man appeared surprised at her insightfulness. But Gabriel did not seem surprised, merely interested. And that was not typical. Men in Andrea's experience never actually liked women who thought. Either all men in Spain thought differently, or it was just Gabriel. She looked at the man in front of her, now telling some story involving a ship and a horse, and she decided it was just Gabriel who was different.

* * *

"I would speak with you, Andrea."

Ademar stood awkwardly at the edge of the courtyard. For once, he did not have any papers with him, nor was he rushing off to the port or hiding in his office. He twisted the gold ring on his thumb, a sure sign he did not wish to be there.

Andrea smiled at him, hoping that would put her father at ease. This was his first time seeking out her company, and while she welcomed it, she also could not help but wonder why now. She had not made any overt missteps at the ball, and Luisa's invitations were becoming more frequent, so he could not be upset with how her entry into society was going. She shook herself. Perhaps he only wished to spend the day with her.

"Good afternoon, Papa," she smiled bracingly.

"Did you enjoy yourself at Don Sebastián's ball?" Ademar asked, more out of a sense of politeness than of real interest.

"I did. It was all quite beautiful and different from what I am used to at home."

"This is your home now, Andrea," Ademar replied sharply.

"Of course, Papá. I did not mean," Andrea did not say anything more. Spain may be her home now, but it did not feel that way yet.

"How old are you now?" he asked, changing the subject.

"Twenty."

Ademar pursed his lips. Apparently, twenty was old. "Well, it is past time for you to have a husband. You are my daughter, so there should be no trouble finding someone suitable. Indeed there is already interest," he hesitated, "but there will be time for that later."

Andrea shivered, suddenly cold. Marriage? But she had only just arrived. Her father never mentioned a word about marriage before this, and now he spoke of her making a splendid match with no talk of the interested suitor, as though Andrea's preferences did not matter. She missed her mother, who had spoken softly of a love that overcame all barriers. And look how well that ended, she thought bitterly.

Don Ademar regained his daughter's attention. "All of Sevilla watched you at the ball, and they will watch you at every party you attend. I want you to remember you are Spanish now. There will be no talk of New Spain or your family and life there."

Andrea bowed her head.

# Eleven

*"The truth may be stretched thin, but it never breaks, and it always surfaces above lies, as oil floats on water." - Miguel de Cervantes, Don Quixote*

"I have been hearing rumors, Gabriel," Daniela said sternly, a frown marring the smooth plane of her forehead.

She was waiting for him when he came home, tapping her foot with impatience as a footman took his coat and hat and then wisely made himself scarce. Before he could say a word, Daniela ushered him into the front parlor where she regally perched herself upon a couch and somehow still managed to look down her nose at him even though he remained standing by the door. How did mothers always seem to make one feel like he was still a schoolboy?

He caught himself shifting on the balls of his feet and immediately went to sit down. It was better to look at his mother in the eye. Gabriel could hold his own in front of the King and his advisors, but his mother was a force to be reckoned with on a completely different scale. To put it bluntly, she scared the hell out of him.

Take now, for instance. Daniela looked like a porcelain doll, although anyone who knew her could tell you that beneath her delicate beauty lay an indomitable will and fierce spirit. Gabriel recognized the pursed lips and narrowed eyes. She may not like to admit it, but whatever these rumors were, she was concerned.

"Yes, Mamá?"

"It has come to my attention that you have been calling upon Doña Andrea de Piña."

"Has it?" he asked casually.

"Yes, it has," she said testily. "My friends can speak of little else it seems."

"I offer the girl my patronage, take her shopping, and make sure her first ball was a success, and then nothing! You have not mentioned her once. My friends have to tell me you are courting her."

"I see what this is," Gabriel crossed his arms, a laugh escaping him at Daniela's huff of impatience. "You are upset because you are not involved."

She sniffed at him, not commenting one way or the other, but Gabriel knew he was right. His mother's feelings were hurt that he might be interested in a woman and she did not know.

"Mamá," he walked over to the couch and sat down next to her. He felt large and awkward on the dainty sofa, no doubt Daniela's intention when she furnished the parlor. She always liked to have the upper hand. He gathered her hand in his. "I have no intention of marrying Doña Andrea. I admit I have been in her company, but that is because I am working with her father, and we are frequently thrown into each other's company. If I were truly courting a lady, you would be the first to know."

Throughout the course of his work as an agent, he had learned to ignore any feelings of discomfort, so it was easy enough to overlook the current twinges in his chest. There was a foreign feeling swirling around in there, but he ignored it.

Daniela narrowed her eyes at him, gauging his sincerity. Whatever she saw satisfied her, for she merely patted his hand and called for coffee.

\* \* \*

Gabriel ducked down into an alleyway, narrowly missing two dockworkers. The roughspun cotton rubbed against his skin. It was too small, procured by his valet who protested dressing Gabriel in poor quality clothing by making sure it did not fit properly. He made a mental note to allow Manolo free reign with his clothing tomorrow.

He slowed down, cautiously approaching the warehouse that belonged to Don Ademar de Piña. It was a typical warehouse, with offices on the second floor, and a large holding space that could fit the cargo of multiple galleons. Most merchants hired one or two men to guard their buildings at night, but Gabriel counted seven men patrolling Ademar's building. That alone would not raise Gabriel's suspicions, not if there was valuable cargo inside, but he had it on good authority that Ademar was not expecting a new shipment for at least a fortnight.

There was no question then. Gabriel had to get closer. Ademar made it difficult to search his office, but he had not seen anything of much interest during a preliminary search, so the logical next place to look was his warehouse. There must be something of importance if that many guards were here. He would search the offices, check the contents of the cargo against his list of missing items, and then be finished with the whole de Piña family, Andrea included. It was the only way.

And with that, Gabriel got to work. Glancing around a convenient wall, he waited until the two guards at the side door split up, walking in opposite directions on a patrol route. He took a deep breath and simply walked up to the door. His experience had shown him that if he acted as if he belonged, people would rarely question him. That is not to say, however, that he did not walk as quickly as possible without running. He may like to take risks, but he was not stupid.

Looking left and right, he gingerly tested the door. Locked. He pulled slim tools out of a pouch at his belt, crouching in front of the door. Gabriel bit his lip as he worked, quickly inserting the long piece of metal into the lock. Another tool joined it, this time with a slight hook at the end. He jostled them about, searching for the latch.

"But the ale is cheaper at Mario's," a voice protested.

"Yes, but the women are prettier at Cruz's," a second voice joined the first.

Gabriel stiffened. Damn. That patrol went by rather quickly. He redoubled his efforts, breathing deeply and keeping his hands steady as the footsteps drew nearer.

His shoulders relaxed as the locked opened with a faint click. He pushed the door open a crack, and slid in, the door closing just as the guards returned to their post. He would not be leaving from that door. The lock picking tools silently went back into their pouch, and Gabriel got to work.

He quickly made his way across the floor, to climb the stairs that lead to the offices. There were no lights except the flickering torches of the guards outside, but the moon was with him tonight and the second-floor windows let in enough light for him to get by. The desk here was similar to Ademar's desk at home – covered in stacks of papers.

Making sure the office door was closed behind him, Gabriel moved to the desk and began looking through the documents. His eyes narrowed, roving down the pages, skimming them for anything incriminating or anything different from what Ademar kept in his office.

They were mostly innocuous documents, containing crew lists and berth requests at each port along the fleet route. There were letters from representatives in Veracruz and Havana and even a letter that looked to be from Ademar's lawyer. Interesting, but not what he was looking for. Gabriel flipped to the next page.

And there it was.

It was an accounting list from a Manolo Vasquez, a clerk from the *Casa de Contratación* Gabriel knew for a fact did not exist. This Manolo listed cargo from the *Santa María*, the next galleon scheduled to arrive from Veracruz. Ademar had not yet given him a cargo list for the *Santa María*, because it was supposed to arrive with the ship in another two weeks.

Gabriel knew he could not take the list with him, so he rummaged through the desk drawers until he found a blank piece of paper. He picked up a quill still resting in the inkpot at the edge of the desk, and began to copy the document. Writing quickly, he waved the paper in the air for the ink to dry before folding in and placing it in his pouch with his other things.

Aside from almost being spotted on his way out the door, Gabriel made his way out of the warehouse as easily as he made it in. If it would not have brought unwanted attention, he would have whistled all the home, because his mission was finally moving forward. It may have been past 4 o'clock in the morning when Gabriel returned to his house, but he went to sleep with a smile.

# Twelve

*"I know who I am and who I may be, if I choose."* - Miguel
de Cervantes, Don Quixote

Andrea picked at her usual breakfast of fruit and pastries, her
appetite fleeing as she stared at the other end of the long table.
Ademar's chair sat empty, as it did every day. After that first
day, she had taken to eating breakfast in the dining room, hoping to catch a glimpse of Ademar. Either he was avoiding her,
or he rose much earlier in the morning than she did. Two footmen hovered about the sides of the dining room in the red livery
she had come to recognize as her family's. They looked straight
ahead, not speaking, though she knew they would pour her more
coffee the instant her cup ran low.

She could pour her own coffee and make up her own plate, of
course, but after the acute dismay on the footman's face the first
time she tried to put together her breakfast, Andrea decided to
ignore her discomfort at being served and to enjoy the luxury. As
María had explained, serving food was part of their duties, and
they found pride in their work.

One of the footmen stepped forward with the coffee pot, pouring the drink into her now empty cup. She smiled and thanked him before stirring in a small amount of sugar. The dining room door opened as he set the pot back onto the sideboard. Andrea ignored it, thinking it was probably another servant walking in. She took a sip of her coffee, nearly burning her tongue at the heat.

Coughing into her napkin, she missed the footmen snapping to attention. By the time she sat back in her chair, the seat across from her was filled. Ademar sat there, reading the paper as one footman prepared a plate and another filled his cup. This marked the first time Ademar had joined her for breakfast since her arrival in Sevilla, and she did not know what to do.

She waited for him to look up, to say something, anything, but he merely turned the page. It was up to her then, to erase this distance between them.

Andrea cleared her throat.

"Good morning, Papá."

The rustling stopped. Bright green eyes, so like her own, peered at her over the top of the paper.

"Good morning, Andrea," he replied after a pause.

She waited for him to continue, to ask after her sleep or inquire about her plans for the day, but nothing. He returned to his reading, his greeting seemingly enough after weeks of not seeing her. She tried to swallow her impatience, she really did, but restraint was not her strong suit. For heaven's sake, she had been in Spain for almost a month and she could count the number of times she had spoken to her father on one hand. They lived in the same house, and never saw each other! Not for the first time, she questioned her decision to come to Spain.

"I am attending a dinner party at Luisa's tonight. Will you be joining me?" A little blunt, perhaps, but at least it guaranteed an answer.

Ademar speared a piece of apple with a fork. He looked at it carefully, inspecting it for any brown spots. Satisfied, he placed the apple in his mouth, chewed, and swallowed, taking his time all the while.

Andrea's foot tapped impatiently, though silently, and she gripped her hands together underneath the table.

"At the del Toro's?" he asked.

"Yes, her mother is hosting."

"Hmm, I do not think so. There is too much work to do. Give my regards to Doña Luisa and her family. It is good you are friends with them, they are good connections to maintain."

Andrea felt a stab of disappointment that she would be going alone. Nevertheless, she tried one more time to engage her father in conversation.

"May I ask what you are working on?" she asked, hoping her formality would encourage him to speak. Ademar did not inspire any sort of comfortable conversation. How had her mother ever fall in love with him? Although she supposed with the language difference Ademar's conversation did not matter. She refused to think of how easy it was talking with Gabriel, how their conversations seemed to flow so naturally and with such ease. She never suffered through uncomfortable silence with him.

"My ship, the *Santa María*, arrives in port today. All the preparations for her arrival need to be finalized."

Andrea nodded, so surprised he answered her question that it took her a moment before asking another one.

"What kind of preparations?"

Ademar had already returned to his newspaper, but at this, he put it down for the first time since sitting at the table. He looked suspiciously at her as if suddenly realizing it was Andrea he was speaking to, and not a business associate.

"It does not concern you," he said sternly, dismissing her.

"Of course, Papá. I was merely curious." Andrea nodded to the nearest footman, who walked over to pull out her chair. She stood and curtsied to her father who did not see it. At the door, she turned back around and looked at Ademar. His head was bowed, so engrossed in his reading that his coffee had surely by now grown cold, the rest of his breakfast untouched.

"Have a good day, Papá," she said, with more than a hint of wistfulness.

He did not answer.

With no plans for the day until the dinner party that night, Andrea decided to borrow a book from her father's library and read outside in the courtyard. She had found a volume of poetry that she wanted to finish, and it would be the perfect distraction. She did not want to spend the rest of the day alternating between nervousness about the party and disappointment about her father.

Shawl in hand to protect against the chill in the shade, she settled herself in the metal chair. She had requested cushions the last time she had been here, and she was pleased to see that they made the metal chair much more comfortable. The courtyard was quickly becoming her refuge, and she wanted it as comfortable as possible. By her estimate, she had hours upon hours before María would collect her to prepare for dinner, so she settled in to read.

The hours passed by far too quickly, and she had just turned to the last page when María shook her shoulder exasperatedly. "Doña!" by the tone of her voice, it was far from the first time María had tried to gain her attention. The maid looked frazzled, so Andrea closed the book without complaint.

"Oh, dear, I am sorry María," Andrea apologized as she stood and stretched. "I suppose I was lost in the words. Is the day already gone?"

"Yes, Doña, you have been out here all day." María clucked like a mother hen as she ushered Andrea inside. "I have laid out your dress for tonight, but first you must bathe."

They climbed the stairs quickly as María went on about the preparations necessary for tonight. It almost seemed more involved than her preparations for the ball, but at least this way Andrea was certain to look the part. She thought about that as she washed in warm, soapy water scented with lavender. Except for knowing very few people, she blended in at the ball. No one accused her of not belonging, and although they knew she was from New Spain, no one thought she was anything other than Spanish.

She hoped the same held true for tonight.

Tonight there would be more pressure. There would be fewer people, and she would have to make more polite conversation about society things that she did not know. She would need to guard her tongue against any slip-ups, for it would not do to appear as anything other than a marqués' daughter. Hopefully, she would be sitting near Luisa, so her friend could help her out of any troublesome questions.

María handed her a towel, and she dried off, pulling a silk chemise over her head. Even bathing was different here. Her bathwater was scented with roses, and her chemise was finer silk than any she had sold in her shop. Living in Spain came with plenty of adjustments, but wearing silk was an adjustment she made happily. She wrapped herself in a dressing gown and then sat down in front of her vanity table. She brushed her hair as María cleaned away the bath and summoned a maid to take away the dirty towels.

"All right, I am ready," Andrea declared.

"Good." María stood behind Andrea, pursing her lips in thought. She picked up Andrea's hair, pulling it back experimentally. "Off the face, I think."

She spent the next twenty minutes pinning and twisting Andrea's hair into an elegant chignon. Andrea could not see what it looked like in the back, but María's smug look as she secured a final hairpin guaranteed its perfection. It was too bad María could not come with her to the dinner.

Andrea stood, then stepped into her dress, careful not to dislodge any of María's hard work. As María laced her corset, Andrea gently rubbed the fabric between her fingers, testing its quality. It was a beautiful dress, a deep blue with delicate lace trim around the bodice. She breathed in sharply as María tugged her corset even tighter than normal.

"How am I supposed to eat wearing this?" Andrea complained. She could barely breathe, let alone fit anything in her stomach. Her ribs protested their confinement, and she pressed her hand ineffectually against her bodice.

"Ladies do not eat," María responded as if she said nothing out of the ordinary.

"What?"

"It's true. At a dinner like this, you will take only a few bites of each course."

"Then what is the purpose of a dinner party?" Andrea asked, quite reasonably to her mind. Why would someone provide food if no one was expected to eat it?

María shrugged. "It provides the opportunity to speak with others in a more intimate setting than a ball." She thought for a moment, then added, "Drink sparingly. The wine may not be watered down, and you may not be used to how strong it is."

Andrea nodded, grateful for the advice. "Thank you, María. I will remember that. And perhaps I may have a tray in my room when I return home?" She smiled cheekily.

"Very well, Doña," María laughed, but nodded. "Now, let us finish dressing you."

# Thirteen

*"Hunger is the best sauce in the world."* - *Miguel de Cervantes, Don Quixote*

Luisa's butler opened the door, welcoming Andrea into a home very similar to her father's in all but décor. Here, a woman's influence was obvious. The colors were lighter, and elegant vases sat upon console tables covered with lace. Candles lit the hallway, providing ample light to see the landscape paintings on the walls. She could see hints of Luisa in the pink pillows in the chairs she spied in an open sitting room and admired a porcelain clock on a narrow table. The home was feminine but tasteful.

Realizing the butler was walking down the hallway without her, she hurried after him. She was embarrassingly out of breath when he left her in the doorway of a different parlor with a bow. Andrea took a deep breath to steady her pulse, and with a confidence she did not feel, stepped into the room.

Luisa saw her right away and hurried over, arms outstretched in welcome. "I am so happy you are here!" She hugged Andrea tightly. "You will never guess who is here. Mamá is beside herself with joy."

Curious, Andrea followed Luisa over to Doña Carolina del Toro, Luisa's mother, who did indeed look very pleased with herself.

"Doña Carolina," Andrea curtsied, "thank you so much for inviting me."

The older woman smiled indulgently. "Of course my dear. We are so pleased you were able to attend. We will be going in to dinner soon, but please have a drink."

Social obligations completed, Luisa impatiently pulled Andrea to the side. "The Marquesa de Silva is here," Luisa leaned in and lowered her voice, "and she brought her son the Marqués."

Gabriel was here? Andrea looked around quickly at the small gathering of people before catching herself. It would not do to look overeager.

Gabriel stood next to his mother, talking with two other men. Rather, his mother spoke and he looked bored. He was dressed simply, as was his habit, in a doublet and hose that seemed all the more elegant for their lack of adornment. By comparison, the other men, a mere *vizconde* and *barón*, looked like they were trying much too hard. Gold dangled from their ears and dripped from their fingers, but they eyed Gabriel enviously.

Eyes so dark as to be almost black met hers. Andrea broke the eye contact with a gasp and looked away. Utterly embarrassed at being caught staring, her blush spread as she kept looking over at Gabriel's knowing smirk. A curious sense of dread grew in her stomach as he excused himself from the group and slowly walked toward her. Torn between wanting to flee and wanting to speak to him, she bounced on the balls of her feet. The dread morphed into something undecipherable the closer he came.

"Doña Andrea, how delightful to see you. Doña Luisa." He bowed to them both, though his eyes remained on Andrea.

He raised his glass to his mouth, though it did nothing to cover his smug look.

Andrea curtsied, head down, hoping it would give her a moment to recover her composure. A hopeless endeavor, for she had never learned to hide away her emotions. She wished for a smidgeon of Luisa's way with society and men.

"Doña Luisa is a particular friend of mine, Marqués. Her family was kind enough to invite me." There. That sounded poised enough.

She need not have worried, however, for Gabriel had already turned to her friend.

Luisa was giggling at something he said, and his grin turned satisfied. Out of the corner of her eye, she saw a footman about to walk past her. To keep herself from throwing something out of irrational jealousy, she turned toward him and grabbed a glass from his tray. Ignoring his startled face, she mumbled a thanks, and quickly took a large gulp. The wine did nothing to relieve the feeling that had moved to her chest, and she desperately took another sip.

Gabriel was still flirting with Luisa, and as she wondered if she should leave them to it, a hand touched her elbow. Gabriel's mother stood beside her, watching her son with some amusement.

"He is just like his father," Daniela said fondly, shaking her head with a laugh. "I would not blame you a bit if you did not speak to him for the rest of the evening."

"Wh-what?" Andrea blanched, hoping she had not been as obvious as all that.

"Oh my dear," the other woman looked at her sympathetically, "you look as though you swallowed something quite horrible."

Andrea grimaced, ready to deny everything. She had no reason to be jealous of Luisa. Gabriel was free to pay his attentions to any lady he wanted. She did not like him in that way, even if he was the most handsome man she had ever seen. Although why he must flirt with her only friend, she had no idea. She liked Luisa, really she did, but she could not deny that her friend was beautiful and charming, and knew this life much better than Andrea did. Luisa would be a good match for Gabriel. Andrea took another sip of wine to hide the grimace twisting her lips.

"You are mistaken, Marquesa, the wine is simply stronger than I am used to." It was a weak defense, but it was the only she could come up with on such short notice. She had no claim on Gabriel, and she was certainly not interested in him, no matter how attractive he may be.

"When Gabriel was a boy, he followed his father around like a puppy. Carlos was the most charming man, but I think even he would have met his match in our son." Daniela laughed, a sound tinged with sadness.

"If you do not mind my asking, Marquesa, how did he die?"

"A hunting accident. Carlos rode quite well but, well, there was an accident, and an infection set in." She shrugged her shoulders fatalistically, although it obviously upset her still.

"I am so sorry. Your loss, and the Marqués', must have been devastating. It is good you have each other." Andrea laid her hand upon Daniela's arm, hoping to provide some kind of comfort.

It worked, for Daniela perked up a little, and patted Andrea's hand. "You will be good for him, I think," she said simply.

"Oh I do not, that is I have no intention -"

Daniela smiled. "We shall see."

Andrea glanced automatically at Gabriel, and the pressure in her chest began to ease. She would have said more when a cough sounded from the doorway.

"Attention everyone. Dinner is ready," Carolina announced.

Here was another source of panic. She did not know the rules for this. Who was her escort into the dining room? Where was she supposed to sit? She looked around for Luisa, but she was already arm in arm with the Marqués de Figueroa and walking into the dining room. Turning to Daniela in a panic, she was about to ask what she should do when Gabriel stepped before them both, followed by the Conde de Vigo. The conde offered his arm to Daniela, who smiled encouragingly back at her as they walked from the room.

"Shall we?" Gabriel offered her his arm, his face suspiciously blank. It seemed he was much better at concealing his thoughts than she.

"Of course." She rested her hand on his arm, trying – and failing – to ignore how the muscle tensed under her fingers. His arm was solid under her hand, and she took strength from it.

He lead her from the parlor, across the hallway, and then into the dining room where the party took their seats. Andrea gasped.

She had never before seen such an elegant table. The table was as large as the one at her home, but it was laden with gold-rimmed plates and elegantly cut crystal glasses. On each end and at the middle sat tall candelabras, the silver polished to a mirror-like gleam. Smaller flower arrangements sat at their bases, adding pops of bright blues and pinks. The candlelight reflected softly on the guests, flickering over white lace tablecloth. Tall footmen of equal height lined the walls on either side of the table, wearing matching livery and white gloves, ready to begin serving the meal at Doña Carolina's signal.

Gabriel pulled out her chair. A footman appeared to pour her more wine. A second footman immediately replaced him to serve her the first course. She took a small sip of her soup once her hostess had begun and conversations started up around her. Peeking at Gabriel, he appeared perfectly at ease, but she knew it was a young lady's responsibility to converse with her dinner partner. María may not have gone over all the rules for dining with company, but that was the one she emphasized the most.

She wracked her brain for something interesting to say, but her knack for conversing had gone out the window it seemed. She and Gabriel never lacked for things to talk about, but tonight was different somehow. Perhaps it was the way the candlelight softened the planes of his face, or the people pretending not to watch them, but Andrea felt more out of place than ever. He should be sitting with Luisa, or one of the other women at the table. They were beautiful, and fully Spanish, and comfortable speaking with handsome men at dinner parties. If she were as Spanish as she looked, she would know what to say to the man sitting beside her.

The seconds dragged on, stretching to eternity, and Gabriel, at last, took pity on her. "My father used to breed horses," he said companionably.

"Really?"

Gabriel smiled at her eagerness. Hoping he did not assume her interest was solely due to relief, she continued. "I love horses, they are such lovely creatures." She winced at her clumsy wording, but Gabriel did not seem to care.

"They are, are they not? My first memory is that of a horse. I think my father put me on a pony as soon as I could walk."

Andrea raised her eyebrows skeptically. "That seems very young," she commented.

"It is, but that is our way. That pony and I went everywhere together."

She smiled, picturing it.

"Does your mother enjoy riding as well?" Andrea asked as the footmen removed the soup bowls, and served the second course.

"She does. We ride through the park every week."

"You are a dutiful son."

Gabriel looked a little sheepish. "Nonsense. I simply go where I am commanded."

"I think there is more to it than that. The Marquesa speaks very fondly of you."

"Ah, so you do speak of me. I wondered." A brilliant grin flashed over his face. "You know," he continued cheekily, "you are very pretty when you blush. You should do it more often."

"I seem to be constantly red around you," she responded, flustered. "Are you always this, this bold?"

Gabriel picked up his wineglass and swirled the ruby liquid

inside. He stared at it, unblinking, for so long she thought he would not respond. After a full minute, he broke the silence. "No."

It almost took Andrea a moment to remember what he meant. Somehow she managed a light laugh. "I do not know if I believe you," she said. Inwardly, she was impressed with herself. It was almost as if she were flirting.

"Well I am certainly not timid, but I am not usually this, ah, forward." He looked almost surprised as he spoke as if he had not known this about himself before.

"Then I suppose I shall be flattered," she said primly, blotting her mouth with her napkin.

"It was a compliment," he confirmed graciously.

His suspiciously blank face only increased her discomfort, and she steered the conversation back to safer waters. She was not that talented in the art of flirtation.

"Did you know I have never ridden a horse before?" She sighed with relief as he took the bait.

"Never?" He gaped at her, appalled. "How can you have never ridden a horse?"

"Please, I beg of you, not so loudly." She reached her hand out pleadingly. "It is my shameful secret," she laughed playfully.

"Very well," Gabriel said with mock gravity. "It shall be our secret."

"Good." Andrea nodded, turning back to her dinner.

"But," Gabriel continued slowly. "if you wish to learn, I could teach you?" He almost looked anxious for her response.

She looked at him thoughtfully.

"Only if you wish it," he finished hurriedly.

A wide smile gave him her answer.

\* \* \*

Gabriel carried the memory of Andrea's smile with him the next day as he visited his horse, Trueño, in the stable behind his house. The stable was his favorite place in the city, a place he went to whenever he needed a boost of comfort or encouragement. He breathed in the scent of oats, listened to the whinnies of the horses, and felt the rough wooden panels of the stalls under his palms. It helped him feel close to his father who had died years earlier, but whose absence was always felt. Sometimes days would go by without thinking of the former marqués, but then he would look at a book his father read once or sit in the same chair in his mother's parlor, and the loss would hit him anew. They shared a love of horses, and Trueño had been a gift when Gabriel entered into the king's service. The two had been on many missions together, and each time it was like his father went with them.

Trueño nudged his shoulder, snuffling gently over the door to his stall. It would be embarrassing to ever admit it out loud, but the black horse was his best friend. Gabriel reached into his jacket pocket and pulled out an apple. He held it out to Trueño, who grabbed it with his teeth eagerly and retreated his head back into his stall.

"I see how it is," Gabriel laughed. "You only want me for food."

Trueño bobbed his head in agreement.

"Don Gabriel?" An ostler hovered nearby, holding a bucket filled with brushes. "Shall I ready your horse?"

"No, Mateo, I will groom Trueño myself." Gabriel dismissed the ostler, taking the bucket from him.

Stepping into the stall, Gabriel took the curry brush and began brushing his horse's neck. Gabriel thought about his mission as he worked, the strokes of the brush a meditation.

"I know he is smuggling, there was enough at the warehouse to support that. But I have found nothing to suggest Don Ademar is keeping anything here in Sevilla. It is not at his warehouse I know that. So where could it be?"

Trueño sighed as Gabriel moved to brush the horse's other side.

"You are right. I will keep looking. It will turn up. It must."

Gabriel finished brushing Trueño, and stood at his head, scratching between the horse's ears. He was tense. For some reason, the stable was not as restorative as it usually was for him. This case was particularly troublesome, and all because of a pair of green eyes.

# Fourteen

"*The truth may be stretched thin, but it never breaks, and it always surfaces above lies, as oil floats on water.*" - *Miguel de Cervantes, Don Quixote*

Andrea glanced both ways before slipping through the door, barely open a crack. She pulled her skirts in after her and shut the door with a quiet click. It was time to discover what Ademar spent all his time on, and what she was not allowed to see. If she weren't afraid of discovery she might have laughed at how, if only her father had taken a little more interest in her, she would not be here rifling through his desk drawers. As it was, she was going to learn more about him the only way she could.

She may not know anything about ships or the *Casa de Contratación*, but what she did know was numbers. And the quickly calculated columns on the sheet in her hands were not adding up. Silver, hemp, dyes, spices, and more were listed as cargo for the *Santa María*. She had no idea what a galleon's typical cargo was worth, but after managing a store with her mother, she knew how much dyes and textiles cost. Indigo and black dyes were much more costly than other dyes and than what was listed on the cargo log. Hemp would also cost more. It was a growing export, but even in a large quantity, it would be the same price as the linen listed farther down the page. The bottom corner was covered in a large seal, the mark of the Casa de Contratación. This type of cargo log must be how they calculated the tax owed to the king.

Setting the log to the side, Andrea moved to the next drawer. She tried to pull it open, but it was stuck. Using both her hands this time, she pulled harder, gritting her teeth with effort as it slid open. It was shallower than the other drawers. Andrea stuck her hand in, searching the back to see if something was blocking it. Nothing. Just the back of the drawer. Inches from where it should end. She could not stop the excited giggle that escaped her as she dug her fingernails into the line where the bottom of the drawer met the back. She flinched as a nail bent backward, but any pain faded into the background when the piece of wood gave way, exposing the rest of the drawer. She set it aside, careful not to disturb anything on the desk.

The first roll of paper unrolled easily as she picked it up. Andrea gasped. It was a list of the *Santa María*'s cargo but, she checked it quickly against the list she had found earlier, it did not match. Eyes scanning over the page, these prices seemed more accurate. At least, the prices for the dye looked right, she could not be sure about the rest. The total number of pesos was much larger on this list than on the one she had already found. Her gaze dropped to the corner. There was no seal.

Suspicions started twirling in her mind. What did this mean? Why would Ademar change the value of a cargo? She took a deep breath, rubbing at the tightness in her chest that was getting worse the longer she stayed in the study. It was much too risky taking anything out of the room, but she looked hard at the documents, comparing them.

"80,000 pesos, not 60,000 pesos. 80,000, not 60,000," she repeated over and over, memorizing the figures.

She jumped in fright as the front door opened, and she faintly heard Francisco's deep voice asking her father if he wished for any food or drink. She could not make out Ademar's response, but it was time to go before he discovered her in his office. She wanted her father's attention, but not like this. The voices were getting louder, so Andrea quickly shoved the papers in the drawer, replacing the covering at the back. She ran across the room, thinking invisible thoughts, stopping when she reached the door. Taking in the room at a glance, everything looked as Ademar had left it. Hopefully.

Only when she was back in her room did she feel she could take a breath.

* * *

Gabriel looked at the note in his hands. Manolo, his valet and sometimes butler, had handed it to him with a blank expression. He had received quite a few messages like this while working as an agent of the Crown, so a note in itself was not unusual, but the hint of amusement lurking in Manolo's eyes caught his attention. Reaching the end of the note, he saw why.

"Who delivered this?" Gabriel asked, folding the note and carefully placing it in his shirt pocket.

"A messenger boy wearing the de Piña livery."

"Good." He worried Andrea had delivered it herself. It was unheard of for a young, unmarried lady to write to a man not her betrothed, but at least she had the sense to send someone else. If anyone had seen the de Piña livery, they would simply assume the message was from Don Ademar. That was fine with Gabriel.

Andrea wrote that she had found something she could not speak to her father about and wondered if he, as her father's business associate, would speak to her and give her advice. Gabriel found his one piece of actual evidence and called for his horse, Trueño. He reached the de Piña house in record time.

"Good afternoon, Marqués de Silva. Shall I inform Don Ademar you are here?" Francisco asked after Gabriel had stepped inside.

"No, I am here to see, ah, Doña Andrea," Gabriel responded a little sheepishly.

"Of course, Marqués," Francisco said with no change of expression. "Right this way."

Francisco led the way down the hallway to the courtyard Gabriel was growing as familiar with as Ademar's study. Andrea looked up as he stepped out the door. He swallowed, struck anew by her direct stare.

He was starting to feel guilty, an unusual feeling for him. He never expected to like Andrea. The king all but forbid him to grow attached to the daughter of the man he was investigating. It was those eyes of hers, Gabriel mused. He had a weakness for green eyes. Apparently. But her intelligence impressed him, and she knew more of the world than the dainty Spanish ladies of his acquaintance. He could speak to her of more than idle gossip, and she gave her opinion without attempting to entrap him into a proposal. She acted too forthrightly to be coquettish and was too naive to ever suspect he might spy on her using his connections. Protocol demanded he keep his investigations secret, but he wanted to confide in her. She remained ignorant of her father's actions, but she was unprepared for the consequences he would face when Felipe moved against him.

The king would not appreciate his breach of secrecy, but Gabriel reasoned that telling Andrea the truth was the only way to find out where Ademar had secreted away his treasure. Andrea found something, and she needed him to confirm her suspicions. With luck, he would find the treasure and confiscate it for Felipe. And then this would be his last mission as an agent. He had decided. He was too old for such things, and the innocent face in front of him was giving him ideas of a future.

Andrea rose, a wide smile on her face as she curtsied.

"Gabriel!" She blushed, realizing she had used his first name. "I mean, Marqués de Silva."

A tightness in his chest did not know was there loosened. He rubbed at it absently. His name had never sounded so good. He smiled back at her, "Doña Andrea. I came as soon as I got your note."

She sat down, gesturing for him to sit across from her. Taking a deep breath, she explained.

"I found something among my father's things, and I am sure it is a simple mistake, but I do not know what to do," she began, twisting her hands in distress.

When she paused, Gabriel asked, "What kind of mistake?"

"I found two cargo lists for the same ship. One was marked

with a seal, but both looked official. I do not believe I would think much of it but," she paused, "they are not exact copies of each other. The totals are different and some of the prices are wrong." Andrea trailed off, clearly uneasy. She lowered her voice and glanced around to see if anyone was listening. "One of the documents was in a hidden drawer."

Gabriel leaned forward. A secret drawer? Falsified documents? It sounded like a story, but this was the break he had been looking for at the warehouse weeks earlier.

"Do you have the documents with you, or are they still in Don Ademar's office?"

"They are in his office. I could not take them out – my father would notice, and I am not supposed to be in there."

He nodded. "What do you remember from them?"

"They were cargo lists for the *Santa María*. One totaled 80,000 pesos and the other 60,000 pesos," she recited.

Gabriel leaped from his chair in his excitement. She had proof. "What else?" he asked eagerly, walking over to her. He almost took her hands in his eagerness, but he restrained himself, barely.

"I am not sure about a lot of it," she said slowly, "but I do know that indigo dye is worth much more than what was listed. And hemp is also worth more."

She looked up at him curiously. "What does this mean? Has my father done something wrong?"

At that, he hesitated. Ademar would be spared the worst punishments by virtue of his rank, but he would be punished. And Andrea would suffer for it.

He pulled his chair next to hers and sat down, his knee brushing against her skirts. "He has been smuggling, and you found the proof."

Andrea's face whitened, and her jaw pulsed with tension. He took one cold hand in his, chafing it to give her some warmth. She took a deep breath but said nothing.

"I never wanted to hurt you," he said. "You will remain untouched by this, I swear it."

She did not seem reassured, and Gabriel knew better than to use more platitudes. She had survived worse than this, and he would trust in her strength of will.

Andrea broke the silence, staring at her hand in his. "How will you get the papers?"

"Let me worry about that. I will get them," he said gently.

"But you need them, do you not?"

"I will take care of it."

She did not look convinced. Gabriel sighed and stood. "I hate to leave you like this, but I must take care of a few things before I speak to your father."

Andrea stood when he did. There was no smile for him now, her happiness at seeing him replaced by worry about her father, even though Gabriel did not think the man deserved her care.

"You will be safe," he promised. He looked carefully at her, deliberately taking her hand. Bringing it to his lips, he kissed it, lingering a moment too long for simple politeness.

She noticed he said nothing about her father's safety.

# Fifteen

*"Take my advice and live for a long, long time. Because the maddest thing a man can do in this life is to let himself die."*
*- Miguel de Cervantes, Don Quixote*

The scream woke her up first. Andrea rubbed her eyes, yawning, stuck in that faraway place between dreams and reality. Her bedroom was dark, only a sliver of moonlight peeking in through the curtains, casting shadows upon the foot of her bed. She lay still, listening. Seconds passed, then minutes. Silence. It must have been a dream, she decided, closing her eyes to sleep again.

"Doña! Doña!"

María threw the door open with a bang and rushed in, her candle flickering in and out due to her speed. The maid's eyes shimmered with tears, her chin wobbled, and the hand clutching her cap trembled. She looked small and very afraid.

Andrea sat up, her long braid tumbling over her shoulder, dread sending tingles down her spine. She clutched anxiously at her blankets.

"What is the matter, María?" she asked, any hope of sleep gone.

"It is your father, Doña. He, he is," María trailed off, tears pouring down her face.

Alarmed, Andrea whipped off the coverlet and stood, grabbing her dressing gown hanging by the foot of her bed. She took María's candle from her grasp, and set it down on the nightstand. She tried to tamp down her impatience and reached out to comfort the obviously distraught girl instead of blurting out questions like she wanted.

María's hands felt like ice. Andrea waited until they began to warm, holding them until she felt María's breathing slow.

"María," she said with a calm she did not feel, "you must tell me what is wrong."

"He is dead! Don Ademar is dead!"

Andrea blinked, reeling as if from a physical blow. Ademar was dead? But she had only just met him. She barely knew him. He may have ignored her, but she had known he was there, down the hall. He was her father. She was here in Spain for him, and now he was dead. He was dead and she was alone. With no money, no way to support herself, and with no family. Oh God, she was alone again.

"Doña?" María asked hesitantly, her tears finally slowing.

"I would see him, María. Where is he?"

"But you cannot! It is not a sight for a young lady."

The idea of a proper Spanish lady's behavior was beginning to grate on Andrea's nerves. But she would not back down. She could not. "Very well," she said. "I will find my father myself."

Andrea brushed María aside and determinedly walked out

into the hallway. It was later than she thought, as sunlight seeped into the windows, splashing red and orange tints on the walls. It did not seem right for there to be a beautiful sunrise while her father lay dead. Francisco hovered nearby, agitation on his usually somber face.

"Doña Andrea," he stood at attention, instantly reverting to his typical behavior. "I am so sorry. May I bring you anything? Tea? Coffee?" Without the flicker of an eyelid, he ignored Andrea's dressing gown, keeping his eyes on her face.

"Just take me to my father, Francisco."

There was a beat before he answered. "Of course, Doña Andrea. He is in his study."

She did not wait to hear more. Rushing down the hallway, she ran down the stairs, anxiety growing as she passed sobbing maids and somber footmen. Tomás, one of the larger and more formidable looking footmen, stood guard outside the study, and she came to a stop in front of him. He looked at her with pity but said nothing as he stepped aside and opened the door for her.

Taking a deep breath, Andrea forced her shoulders down. She remembered Itzel's peaceful passing, the serenity that had passed over her features. The relief that she no longer felt any pain. It was like her mother had fallen asleep. Andrea had survived that, and she would survive this.

Andrea's eyes immediately focused on the hunched figure in the center of the room. Ademar's face looked to the side, slumped over his desk. He looked peaceful for once, the deep grooves in his forehead finally smoothed out by death, his hands relaxed at his sides. The room was dark, the only light coming from outside the office. She stepped closer, taking in the wrinkled velvet doublet and guttered candle next to his head.

She smoothed his hair back, wishing for a moment they could have been this close while he was alive. Maybe he was reunited with Itzel, though Andrea had begun to doubt he thought of her all that much. The movement caught the light, and that is when she saw the blood. Andrea's eyes widened at the large gash at the base of his neck, surrounded by congealed blood. The rusty color as it dried left stains on the doublet, a gruesome decoration. Smothering a cry, her eyes trailed down Ademar's back, to the dark pool underneath his chair. She closed her eyes and turned away, sickened.

It was all she could do to breathe in and out. She must have made a noise because Tomás came in immediately. He carefully avoided looking at the desk, keeping his eyes on her. "Doña?" he asked, unsure of what to do.

"Tea. Please, Tomás," she managed.

"Of course," he bowed his head. "I will have it brought to the parlor right away."

Andrea left the office willingly.

\* \* \*

She was still sitting in the parlor hours later, teacup cold and untouched on the table in front of her. The household remained still, frozen, and she jerked at the sound of a knock on the front door. Francisco's footsteps sounded, and she heard Gabriel's voice moments later. There was a brief silence, and then the parlor door opened.

"Doña, the Marqués de Silva is here to see you. I told him you were unable to receive visitors, but he insisted." Francisco frowned at this breach of manners. It was clear he was unused to being overruled.

Andrea nodded, and he stepped aside to reveal the marqués waiting.

"Doña Andrea," Gabriel strode into the room, the vitality in his stride hurting her eyes. She looked away, seeing her father's prone body in her mind, the contrast between the two men painful.

Gabriel's forehead wrinkled as he took in her drawn, pale face, and a slight tint rose in his cheeks at the sight of her in her nightgown. It was more modest than a ballgown, but she felt completely exposed. She pulled the belt of her dressing gown tighter, her discomfort obvious.

"Are you unwell?"

His gentle tone caught her attention. Andrea raised her eyes to look at him and saw nothing but strength and capability, a body ready to act at any moment. His eyes filled with concern, a concern that grew the more he looked at her distraught expression.

"My father is dead. Killed. I. Well, I am not sure to do now." Her valiant attempt at a smile wobbled before disappearing.

"Good God!" Gabriel immediately sat down next to Andrea, reaching out to take her hand, with no thought to propriety. Her hand was so cold in his. He chafed it gently, holding it between his own. "Has the constable been sent for?"

"No," she said. "I am afraid I, um, that I have just been sitting here."

"You are in shock." He looked over at the full cup of tea and frowned.

He looked around quickly, finding, and ringing the little silver bell on the side table by Andrea's elbow. Francisco, obviously waiting outside the door to be of service to his mistress, opened the door within seconds.

"Yes, Doña?"

"Send for the *Audiencia*," Gabriel ordered. "And have another pot of tea brought in." He looked at Andrea. "Have you eaten anything?"

She shook her head.

"Please bring something to eat as well," Gabriel requested.

Francisco, relieved to have something to do, nodded. He closed the parlor door and called for a messenger before going to the kitchen himself to fetch a tray.

Gabriel scooted closer to Andrea. He hesitated for a moment, wondering how and if he should comfort her. Her blank stare unnerved him. She was not hiding behind stoicism, nor was she putting on a brave face. It was like she wrapped herself in a blanket of ice, and had completely withdrawn.

The woman next to him protected herself. He squeezed the hand he still held tightly. His shoulders were broad enough to take on her troubles, and he would do so gladly.

"We will find out who did this to your father Andrea."

She squeezed his hand back.

# Sixteen

*"Until death it is all life." - Miguel de Cervantes, Don Quixote*

The *corregidor* arrived in no time at all, a summons from the house of a marqués, not one to be ignored. The constable caused such a stir in the servants that Andrea half expected the man to be an imposing giant with intimidating bulk and a dangerous stare that froze suspects in their boots. She silently thanked Gabriel for forcing her to dress. Her skirts and chignon, even her shoes and earrings, armored her against this unknown presence. As did Gabriel, who moved to stand next to her as the parlor door opened and a man stepped inside.

"I am José de Beteta. Where is the body?"

The corregidor was a severe-looking man, with sallow skin and a balding head covered by a hat he had rudely not removed when entering the house. His voice was high pitched, with a nasal quality that sounded as though he were perpetually ill. A small man, his appearance was so different from what she expected that Andrea simply stared.

He wandered through the parlor as though he owned it, rubbing the curtains between his fingers and feeling the crushed velvet of the chairs resting against the walls. He picked up a vase, weighing it in his hands before replacing it on a different shelf than the one he found it on. Francisco looked disapprovingly at him but said nothing.

Gabriel looked at her meaningfully, and Andrea realized he was allowing her to take the lead. He trusted her. Her heart lightened with a pleasure at odds with the situation. Ignoring it, she coughed, returning to the situation at hand.

"It is this way, Corregidor."

Andrea gestured for Beteta to go in front of her, and the group walked down the hallway toward her father's study.

"And you are?" Beteta asked suddenly.

For such a short man, it was remarkable how well he was able to look down his nose at Andrea. They were of a similar height, but Andrea felt quite small indeed in the face of the man's overabundant pride. No introductions had been made, but it should hardly have been necessary. It was her family's house.

"This is Doña Andrea de Piña," Gabriel introduced her, an annoyed expression on his face.

Beteta sniffed, thrusting his nose once more into the air.

"Move," he commanded Tomás, who still guarded the study door, imperiously.

Tomás looked at Andrea first for approval, a gesture of respect that annoyed Beteta, if his flaring nostrils were anything to go by.

She nodded at him, and Tomás stepped aside.

The body was exactly as Andrea had left it – was it only that morning? She felt sick again to see her father lying there so still, and she instinctively looked toward Gabriel for support. He did not notice, however, and was peering around at the study making observations about the scene. It was useless to feel crushed, but Andrea felt an unreasonable disappointment that he was so focused. Beteta meanwhile pulled a notebook out of his coat pocket and began taking notes, muttering to himself.

"There appears to be trauma to the back of the head," Beteta said while circling behind the body. He glanced at the top of the desk and peered underneath the chair. Without looking anywhere else, he suddenly whirled around to face Andrea, pointing his pencil at her. "What did you do with the weapon?" he accused.

Startled, Andrea said, "Weapon? There was no weapon, señor. I did not touch anything, and to my knowledge, neither did the servants."

"Hmm." Beteta pressed his lips together, his disbelief clear.

He continued to look at Don Ademar's body, making notes as he did so and snorting occasionally. He glared once or twice at Andrea and completely ignored Gabriel. Andrea kept her eyes on the ground, unable to look at her father's body, hating to be in his study, but unable to leave the corregidor in there alone. Her eyes strayed to Ademar more than once as she stood there, hugging herself to ease her discomfort.

Meanwhile, Gabriel continued his own investigating. He looked at the books on the shelves, rifling through the papers scattered about the room, but concentrated on the papers on Ademar's desk. Waiting until Beteta's attention was engaged elsewhere, he slipped some of the documents into his pocket to look at more closely later.

"Well, it is obvious that someone killed the señor," Beteta stated arrogantly. "And only I, José de Beteta, can discover the truth."

He paused, before announcing with great drama, "In fact, I already know who is the murderer."

Andrea looked at him in disbelief. It seemed unlikely given her initial impression, but perhaps the man was good at his job. "Who, Señor Beteta?" she asked.

He looked back at her patronizingly. "You of course. You killed Don Ademar." He shrugged fatalistically as though he had not just accused her of patricide. "Everyone knows New Spain is filled with savages, and this was clearly a crime of passion."

"That is enough!" Gabriel interjected with real anger. "Of course she did not kill her father. She would not have the strength for that kind of attack, and furthermore, she is a lady. I demand that you apologize to the Marquesa."

Both Andrea and Beteta jolted at the reminder that she had now inherited her father's position. She was no longer just a marqués' daughter, she was a Marquesa in her own right, and that carried power despite also being a...savage. With that power came protection, something Beteta had overlooked. At least Gabriel did not seem to believe the part of herself left behind in New Spain was bad.

Gabriel continued berating Beteta. "Next time you accuse an innocent, I suggest you provide proof of your suspicions, or I will report you to your superior."

At the mention of proof and the *alcalde mayor*, a truly fearsome man, the good corregidor gulped nervously. "Very well then. I will return later to prove her guilt -" Gabriel glared at him, "- that is to say, to prove the killer's identity," he hurriedly amended his statement.

\* \* \*

"Oh, what an odious little man!" seethed Andrea after Beteta finally left the house after poking his head into every room, taking his time in her bedroom. "He cannot know what he is doing."

She paced rapidly before turning to Gabriel in agitation. "You do believe me, do you not? I did not kill my father."

"Of course you did not," Gabriel reassured her. He looked shocked she even asked.

"Even though I am a savage?" she spit the word out angrily.

"You are a lady," he answered firmly. "Beteta is a mere corregidor. He likely has not dealt with a case like this before, and hopes to prove himself and land a promotion." He absently began following Andrea up the stairs and down the short hallway. "Did you notice anything when you first saw your father's body?" he asked slowly, deep in thought.

"I do not know what I am supposed to have noticed," she sighed. "Nothing remained in the wound, and nothing seemed out of the ordinary."

They reached the end of the hallway, and Andrea opened the door on the right. Gabriel followed her, absently closing the door behind him as he stepped fully into the room. She waited for him to realize where he was, but he either did not notice or did not care.

"You should not be in my bedroom." She arched an eyebrow at him as Gabriel strode across the room to close the curtains.

"Someone might see into your window," he shrugged, ignoring her statement. "I will not take chances with your safety." Apparently, he was paying closer attention than she realized.

"This was no accident, Andrea. Someone murdered your father. If they know about your father's business dealings, they may be looking for the smuggled cargo. In which case, you may be in danger." Gabriel closed the distance between them in a few steps. He needed her to understand she was in trouble. He looked down at her with such intensity that Andrea grew flustered, a blush creeping up her neck.

"Why did you come here this morning, Gabriel?" she asked, stepping out of reach of his arms so she could breathe a little easier.

"I wanted to see you," Gabriel replied a bit sheepishly. "I know it was too early for a social call, but I did not want to arrive and find you had gone out. I wanted to explain."

"Explain what?"

"Your father smuggled cargo out of New Spain. He was a legitimate businessman for the most part," he continued over her protests, "but he falsified documents so that he did not have to pay taxes on his entire shipment."

"Those were the papers I found?"

"Yes."

"Is this my fault? If I never told you about sneaking into his office yesterday, would he still be alive?" she asked pitifully.

"Of course not!" Gabriel rushed to assure her. "No one knew

you found anything or told me anything. Smuggling is danger-ous. This has nothing to do with you."

Andrea looked up at Gabriel, searching his face for answers. He dropped all pretense as he looked back at her, hiding noth-ing, hoping she would listen. She had been intrigued when he told her he worked for the king upon occasion, but with his air of competence in the study, it seemed he worked for the king more frequently than that.

"Was anything you told me true? Did you truly partner with my father?"

He winced, and she knew.

She backed away from him. "You lied to me."

Gabriel opened his mouth, but she overrode him. "Oh I am sure some of it was true, but you lied to me about your work with my father. Is that why you visited me so often? And intro-duced me to your mother? You must have been flattered at how easy it was for me to," she stumbled over her words, but pressed on, "to like you. How you must have laughed at my foolishness."

She had not cried at leaving her home in Mérida, nor at her father's brutal death, but she felt tears on her cheeks now. "Did you ever like me at all?" she asked, wistfully, not truly knowing which answer she hoped for.

Gabriel's mouth opened, but she held up a hand.

"No, do not answer that. Thank you, Marqués de Silva, for being here today, but now I must ask you to leave." She did not wait for an answer but turned her back.

Gabriel's mouth tightened, but he did not protest. He bowed stiffly, murmured "Doña," and quit the room.

For the first time since her mother's death, Andrea collapsed on her bed and cried.

# Seventeen

*"...he who's down one day can be up the next, unless he really wants to stay in bed, that is..." - Miguel de Cervantes, Don Quixote*

The house felt empty after Gabriel left. The servants tiptoed around Andrea's room, carrying on their duties as normal, if more silently. The sunlight pouring through the curtains Andrea had opened sometime during the night was the only sign it was morning. Wincing at her soreness, Andrea uncurled herself and stood, rolling her neck to work out the kinks. She squinted at her reflection in the mirror, which was blotchy and swollen from crying. She poked at the puffy bags under her eyes, sighing. She did not know which was more concerning: that she cried over Gabriel or that she did not cry over Ademar.

Introspection could wait until later, she decided with a tug on the bell pull. Within minutes, María was applying a compress of cold water over her eyes to reduce swelling while Andrea waited for her coffee to cool enough to drink.

"Have there been any messages?" Andrea asked, peeling the compress off one eye to look at the maid.

"Yes, Doña. Many have sent their condolences."

"Nothing else?"

"No, Doña."

"Nothing from the Marqués de Silva? Or any update from the *Audiencia*?" Andrea pressed.

"I could not say specifically, Doña. Francisco has all the correspondence. Shall I ask him?"

"No, no, that's all right María." She would ask Francisco herself.

It was time to stop wallowing and get to work.

She found the butler in the kitchen discussing the dinner menu with the cook. His normally placid face betraying strain. His smooth forehead was heavily creased, and his eyes were filled with worry. Even the cook, normally effusive, was subdued. They both turned to the door when Andrea entered the kitchen. They bowed, and the cook prepared a plate of sliced fruits he immediately placed on the table at which the servants usually ate. He gestured for Andrea to sit, sighing in apparent relief when she bit into a slice of melon.

"Doña Andrea, may I say once again how sorry I am about Don Ademar."

"Thank you, Francisco. I appreciate that." She swallowed the melon and continued. "María informed me I have received some messages. I would like to see them."

"Of course, Doña. They are in the library."

"Excellent." She stood, leaving the rest of the fruit untouched. "Thank you. I shall let you get on with your duties."

Andrea did not know what it was she looked for in the large pile of letters that already cluttered the small desk in the library. It was a smaller version of Ademar's desk in his study, so she picked up a stack of letters at a time until she had carried the entire pile over to an overstuffed leather armchair. She could not bear to sit at the desk. Without bothering to read through each letter, she looked at the bottom of the pages at the signatures, until she came across a name she recognized: Daniela de Silva.

Daniela's note included the standard condolences for Andrea's loss, but a postscript caught her attention. 'Gabriel is quite agitated and implores me to tell you not to worry about your mutual acquaintance, whatever that means. I hope you will inform me if you need anything.'

Andrea folded the letter, placing it at the bottom of the pile. Daniela's note did not surprise her, but the part about Gabriel did. He should have written to her himself, but she supposed he knew just how upset she was with him. Still, she half expected him to walk into the library at any moment despite the early hour. He did not seem the type to sit patiently.

She felt Gabriel's absence more than she did her father's. If she did not know better, she could imagine Ademar was in his study working. Society knew he rarely socialized, so his killer could really be anyone, as they would all expect to find him at his desk. Andrea groaned, thinking of Beteta's incompetence. At least Gabriel would tell her if he found anything. In the meantime, she could not bear to sit here doing nothing. Especially if the corregidor continued to blame her, even if it was for no other reason than her non-Spanish side.

A few of the letters toppled off her lap, and she took a

deep breath, forcibly slowing her shaking. Unclenching her fist, she leaned down to pick up the letters. She might as well read through them. If Gabriel did not make an appearance by the time she finished, she would begin investigating herself.

\* \* \*

"That little rat!" Andrea gasped.

She read through the letter again, hoping she had made some kind of mistake but no, Don Sebastián actually seemed to be courting her via a condolence letter. There was no declaration of affection, rather the feeling that he wanted her father's shipping business. He never called upon her after the ball, as he had requested, spending time in Ademar's office instead. His current words of flattery seemed too obvious a tactic for anything more nefarious than the desire for money.

Deliberately putting him out of her mind, she rang for Francisco.

"Francisco, who found my father in his study?" she asked when he arrived.

"Claudia, the downstairs maid."

"Would you send her to the library? I should like to speak to her."

Francisco nodded. "Of course, Doña. She will be here right away." He bowed, and quietly shut the door behind him.

She placed the letters on the desk before returning to the armchair. She could have sat behind the desk, but she wanted to keep this a conversation, not an interrogation. Hopefully, Claudia could provide some insight into what happened to Ademar.

It was only a few minutes before the maid came to the library. She was a timid thing, with dark hair tightly pulled back into a bun and dark eyes, rimmed red from crying. Her hands worried at an apron, badly creased. Andrea smiled at her, hoping to put the girl at ease, but it only seemed to make her tremble more.

"You are not in any trouble, Claudia," Andrea reassured her.

"Yes Doña," the girl replied, head down. Andrea leaned forward, straining to hear her.

"Please sit down. I have a few questions to ask you about yesterday."

Claudia blanched but sat down on the matching armchair facing Andrea, perched on the very edge.

"Now," Andrea began. "I want you to remember you are not in trouble, but I do need your help. You discovered my father in his study, is that right?"

Claudia nodded.

"Can you tell me exactly what happened?

"*Sí*, Doña. I went downstairs to clean all the rooms. I usually save the study for last because Don Ademar never goes there until after breakfast." A guilty look crossed her face as though she expected Andrea to be angry she didn't clean the study first.

"What time did you come downstairs?" Andrea asked.

"Half past 5, Doña."

Nodding, Andrea gestured for Claudia to continue. "What happened then?"

The maid gulped, before speaking hesitantly. "Don Ademar must have fallen asleep in his office because he was already there when I went in to start the fire and dust. Oh, I am so sorry, Doña!" Tears streamed down Claudia's face. She clutched a handkerchief to her mouth. "I did not know he was dead, I swear! I thought he was sleeping."

"Why do you say he never left his study that night?" Andrea kept her voice soothing and patient as she tried to get the distraught girl to stop crying long enough to answer. She felt very impatient and a little guilty, however, as Claudia kept crying. Even the servants felt more emotion at her father's death!

She took a deep breath and encouraged the girl to do the same. "Claudia," she repeated. "What makes you think Don Ademar never left the study?"

"He was wearing the same clothes he wore when I brought in his dinner tray. And he often works very late."

"When you realized he was not just sleeping, who did you tell?" Andrea's voice was gentle, but inside she was pulsing with energy.

"I told Francisco, and he told Tomás to stand outside the study door so no one else would walk in."

"Thank you, Claudia. That will be all." Andrea dismissed the maid, telling her to take the rest of the day to rest, and leaned back.

Her answers only lead to more questions. Why had Francisco not immediately come to her or send for the *Audiencia*? The household knew Ademar was dead for hours before Andrea woke up. Why had no one awoken her?

Andrea's fingers drummed the armrest of the chair as she sat there lost in thought. If no one came to the house before her father's body was discovered, and he was still in the previous day's clothes, he must have been killed sometime during the night after the maids cleared away his dinner tray and before 5:30 in the

morning. Which meant someone either snuck into the house unnoticed, or the murderer was inside the household.

# Eighteen

*"...he who's down one day can be up the next, unless he really wants to stay in bed, that is..." - Miguel de Cervantes, Don Quixote*

The house felt empty after Gabriel left. The servants tiptoed around Andrea's room, carrying on their duties as normal, if more silently. The sunlight pouring through the curtains Andrea had opened sometime during the night was the only sign it was morning. Wincing at her soreness, Andrea uncurled herself and stood, rolling her neck to work out the kinks. She squinted at her reflection in the mirror, which was blotchy and swollen from crying. She poked at the puffy bags under her eyes, sighing. She did not know which was more concerning: that she cried over Gabriel or that she did not cry over Ademar.

Introspection could wait until later, she decided with a tug on the bell pull. Within minutes, María was applying a compress of cold water over her eyes to reduce swelling while Andrea waited for her coffee to cool enough to drink.

"Have there been any messages?" Andrea asked, peeling the compress off one eye to look at the maid.

"Yes, Doña. Many have sent their condolences."

"Nothing else?"

"No, Doña."

"Nothing from the Marqués de Silva? Or any update from the *Audiencia*?" Andrea pressed.

"I could not say specifically, Doña. Francisco has all the correspondence. Shall I ask him?"

"No, no, that's all right María." She would ask Francisco herself.

It was time to stop wallowing and get to work.

She found the butler in the kitchen discussing the dinner menu with the cook. His normally placid face betraying strain. His smooth forehead was heavily creased, and his eyes were filled with worry. Even the cook, normally effusive, was subdued. They both turned to the door when Andrea entered the kitchen. They bowed, and the cook prepared a plate of sliced fruits he immediately placed on the table at which the servants usually ate. He gestured for Andrea to sit, sighing in apparent relief when she bit into a slice of melon.

"Doña Andrea, may I say once again how sorry I am about Don Ademar."

"Thank you, Francisco. I appreciate that." She swallowed the melon and continued. "María informed me I have received some messages. I would like to see them."

"Of course, Doña. They are in the library."

"Excellent." She stood, leaving the rest of the fruit untouched. "Thank you. I shall let you get on with your duties."

Andrea did not know what it was she looked for in the large pile of letters that already cluttered the small desk in the library. It was a smaller version of Ademar's desk in his study, so she picked up a stack of letters at a time until she had carried the entire pile over to an overstuffed leather armchair. She could not bear to sit at the desk. Without bothering to read through each letter, she looked at the bottom of the pages at the signatures, until she came across a name she recognized: Daniela de Silva.

Daniela's note included the standard condolences for Andrea's loss, but a postscript caught her attention. 'Gabriel is quite agitated and implores me to tell you not to worry about your mutual acquaintance, whatever that means. I hope you will inform me if you need anything.'

Andrea folded the letter, placing it at the bottom of the pile. Daniela's note did not surprise her, but the part about Gabriel did. He should have written to her himself, but she supposed he knew just how upset she was with him. Still, she half expected him to walk into the library at any moment despite the early hour. He did not seem the type to sit patiently.

She felt Gabriel's absence more than she did her father's. If she did not know better, she could imagine Ademar was in his study working. Society knew he rarely socialized, so his killer could really be anyone, as they would all expect to find him at his desk. Andrea groaned, thinking of Beteta's incompetence. At least Gabriel would tell her if he found anything. In the meantime, she could not bear to sit here doing nothing. Especially if the corregidor continued to blame her, even if it was for no other reason than her non-Spanish side.

A few of the letters toppled off her lap, and she took a

deep breath, forcibly slowing her shaking. Unclenching her fist, she leaned down to pick up the letters. She might as well read through them. If Gabriel did not make an appearance by the time she finished, she would begin investigating herself.

* * *

"That little rat!" Andrea gasped.

She read through the letter again, hoping she had made some kind of mistake but no, Don Sebastián actually seemed to be courting her via a condolence letter. There was no declaration of affection, rather the feeling that he wanted her father's shipping business. He never called upon her after the ball, as he had requested, spending time in Ademar's office instead. His current words of flattery seemed too obvious a tactic for anything more nefarious than the desire for money.

Deliberately putting him out of her mind, she rang for Francisco.

"Francisco, who found my father in his study?" she asked when he arrived.

"Claudia, the downstairs maid."

"Would you send her to the library? I should like to speak to her."

Francisco nodded. "Of course, Doña. She will be here right away." He bowed, and quietly shut the door behind him.

She placed the letters on the desk before returning to the armchair. She could have sat behind the desk, but she wanted to keep this a conversation, not an interrogation. Hopefully, Claudia could provide some insight into what happened to Ademar.

It was only a few minutes before the maid came to the library. She was a timid thing, with dark hair tightly pulled back into a bun and dark eyes, rimmed red from crying. Her hands worried at an apron, badly creased. Andrea smiled at her, hoping to put the girl at ease, but it only seemed to make her tremble more.

"You are not in any trouble, Claudia," Andrea reassured her.

"Yes Doña," the girl replied, head down. Andrea leaned forward, straining to hear her.

"Please sit down. I have a few questions to ask you about yesterday."

Claudia blanched but sat down on the matching armchair facing Andrea, perched on the very edge.

"Now," Andrea began. "I want you to remember you are not in trouble, but I do need your help. You discovered my father in his study, is that right?"

Claudia nodded.

"Can you tell me exactly what happened?

"*Sí*, Doña. I went downstairs to clean all the rooms. I usually save the study for last because Don Ademar never goes there until after breakfast." A guilty look crossed her face as though she expected Andrea to be angry she didn't clean the study first.

"What time did you come downstairs?" Andrea asked.

"Half-past 5, Doña."

Nodding, Andrea gestured for Claudia to continue. "What happened then?"

The maid gulped, before speaking hesitantly. "Don Ademar must have fallen asleep in his office because he was already there when I went in to start the fire and dust. Oh, I am so sorry, Doña!" Tears streamed down Claudia's face. She clutched a handkerchief to her mouth. "I did not know he was dead, I swear! I thought he was sleeping."

"Why do you say he never left his study that night?" Andrea kept her voice soothing and patient as she tried to get the distraught girl to stop crying long enough to answer. She felt very impatient and a little guilty, however, as Claudia kept crying. Even the servants felt more emotion at her father's death!

She took a deep breath and encouraged the girl to do the same. "Claudia," she repeated. "What makes you think Don Ademar never left the study?"

"He was wearing the same clothes he wore when I brought in his dinner tray. And he often works very late."

"When you realized he was not just sleeping, who did you tell?" Andrea's voice was gentle, but inside she was pulsing with energy.

"I told Francisco, and he told Tomás to stand outside the study door so no one else would walk in."

"Thank you, Claudia. That will be all." Andrea dismissed the maid, telling her to take the rest of the day to rest, and leaned back.

Her answers only lead to more questions. Why had Francisco not immediately come to her or send for the *Audiencia*? The household knew Ademar was dead for hours before Andrea woke up. Why had no one awoken her?

Andrea's fingers drummed the armrest of the chair as she sat there lost in thought. If no one came to the house before her father's body was discovered, and he was still in the previous day's clothes, he must have been killed sometime during the night after the maids cleared away his dinner tray and before 5:30 in the

morning. Which meant someone either snuck into the house unnoticed, or the murderer was inside the household.

# Nineteen

*"...time has more power to undo and change things than the human will." - Miguel de Cervantes, Don Quixote*

Gabriel left, promising to go directly to court. Andrea found herself relying upon him more and more, finding comfort in his presence and even valuing his connection to the court. She had not forgotten that he misled her with regards to his work with her father, but in light of Ademar's death and the note, it was no longer important. She thought about the note and its demand and suddenly missed her mother with a fierce ache.

She longed for the time, just months earlier, when she had never heard of any treasure. Itzel never mentioned anything about it, and neither had her father. They had never been poor in Mérida, and Ademar's home was truly luxurious, but who knew how much of that was due to his legitimate business? He had to be somewhat legitimate or else he would have no way or opportunity to smuggle. She would doubt that any smuggled treasure existed if not for the note and her father's murder. Enough people believed in its existence for it to have very real effects. And despite everything, she still believed Ademar was a good man. Sure, wealth was a large reason for the Spanish's presence in New Spain, and her very existence was the product of conquest, but Ademar had made her a Spaniard when he did not need to. That had to count for something. She was just not quite sure for what.

Unbidden, Andrea's thoughts turned to Don Sebastián. From the moment she met him in her father's office and later at his ball, he had scared her. She wiped her hand on her skirt, trying to rid herself of her discomfort from his kiss on her hand. She had already scrubbed at it, but the feeling remained. His eyes calculating, he looked at her like he wanted something, something she did not care to speculate on. Brushing her hair, the methodic strokes calmed her, her mind drifting until she straightened with terrible clarity. Don Sebastián asked about her father's time in New Spain at his ball. Could he have killed Ademar? No, she thought. Don Sebastián may make her skin crawl, but he was still a gentleman, a wealthy one at that. He had no need for treasure and no reason to hurt her father.

She put down the brush as someone knocked on the door.

"Come in!"

María opened the door, stepping inside with a steaming cup. "I thought a cup of chocolate might help you sleep, Doña."

"Thank you, María. This is such a nice touch of home," Andrea accepted the cup gratefully.

The warm, rich taste of chocolate reminded her of the evenings she and her mother would sip chocolate and gossip about the customers who visited their shop. Chocolate had been recently brought over to Spain by people like her father, but it had long been used amongst her mother's people, and she was used to drinking a little every night. Each bitter sip strengthened her, warming her body like a hug, reminding her she was not wholly alone.

"Do you need anything else, Doña?" María asked.

"This is perfect. Thank you, María." Andrea stretched out a hand, taking María's and giving it a gentle squeeze. María looked startled but gave her a small smile before bobbing a curtsey.

"Goodnight, Doña Andrea."

Andrea slowly sipping her chocolate, savoring each taste before the cup was empty. She could not say she was happy, but she slipped into bed in a decidedly better mood, feeling more positive than she had in days. She would have to request more chocolate tomorrow. She blew out the candle and lay back against the soft pillows, pulling the covers up to her chin. Sleep had proved elusive the last few days and she did not expect to sleep, but she quickly drifted off, dreaming dreams of the twinkling eyes and warm smiles of her partner in crime.

*  *  *

The next morning Gabriel found himself, once again, riding to the palace on business. Even Trueño stepped with more energy than usual. It amazed him that he went eagerly, without his usual procrastination, although he supposed it should not surprise him. The desire to be useful to a beautiful woman was a strong motivation. Indeed, he marveled at the changes Andrea had wrought in him already. He found himself thinking more about the future than he used to, a future without sneaking into warehouses and roleplaying, a future where his visits to court only came about because of social obligations. A future he could no longer imagine without Andrea in it.

She was everything he wanted, but never hoped to wish for. She challenged him, unafraid, a refreshing change from the women of his acquaintance, and she appeared unaffected by his title. Of course, Andrea was the same rank as he, but that did not seem to weigh with her. If anything, she seemed to think she could order him about.

A chuckle broke from his lips, and he looked around quickly, wiping the tender expression from his face, hoping that no one had witnessed his descent into madness. For it was madness to think of a future with Andrea, a woman who was Spanish but was not at the same time. How could he ask her to be with him, when he did not even know if she wished to remain in Spain when this was all over? She could very easily return to New Spain, taking all of his hope with her. Perhaps, well, perhaps would have to wait until Ademar's killer was found, and the treasure given to the king.

A palace groom approached Gabriel at that moment to take his horse, holding Trueño's bridle as Gabriel dismounted. He nodded to the man, and straightening his shirt sleeves, walked up the palace steps, and through the doors.

Gabriel debated the merits of going directly to the king. This could be considered part of his mission from Felipe, to find the treasure, but his main goal now was to find Ademar's killer. He doubted Felipe would appreciate the difference.

He walked to the archival room instead, the office of one of Felipe's many underlings. The room was empty of people except for a young man seated behind one of the desks. There were four desks in all, each stacked with papers and boxes. Wooden cabinets filled with records of every Spanish territory lined the walls stopping only for the door. The man was probably in his early twenties, with the ink-stained fingers of someone who pored over documents and scribbled notes all day. He hunched over his desk, busy with work. Gabriel cleared his throat, causing the man to look up, finally putting down his pen.

"May I help you?" The man asked, squinting nearsightedly at Gabriel.

"Yes. The king has personally asked me to look into some records for him," Gabriel replied, being purposefully vague. He would rather not share what he was looking for in case Ademar's killer had connections within the palace. It was unlikely, but if he and Andrea were right, and the killer traveled with Ademar from New Spain to Spain, Gabriel could not afford for anyone to know what records he searched. It was better to err on the side of caution.

"Of course, do you know which records?" The man had straightened at the name of the king and was now regarding Gabriel with more than a little awe. It seemed he was determined to be helpful.

"Unfortunately, I do not," Gabriel shrugged. "Would it be all right if I looked around? I will know the records when I find them. I do not wish to keep Felipe waiting," he winked conspiratorially.

The man looked a little taken aback at this break in protocol but luckily did not regard Gabriel with any suspicion. "Of course, Señor. Help yourself. Please let me know if you need any assistance."

Gabriel inclined his head, murmuring his thanks. Taking his time, he started at the corner of the room farthest from the door. He would work his way clockwise until he found what he was looking for. He opened the top drawer of a cabinet and began rifling through the documents. They covered trials, birth and death records, and government appointees. It was clear that these documents had not yet been completely organized.

"How are these records arranged?" Gabriel asked the young man, who had gone back to his scribblings. If there was no system, a search could take days.

The man did not look up or pause in his writing. "As of now, Señor, they are organized by location."

"Thank you," Gabriel replied, turning back to the cabinet.

The records in front of him were all from the Netherlands. This was not the right cabinet. Gabriel closed the drawer with a snap and moved on to the next cabinet. Once again he opened the top drawer and looked at the first document, this time a list of judges in Peru. Sighing, Gabriel moved on. He repeated the process of opening drawers and peering at different pieces of paper until he reached the middle of the room. This time, the documents inside the cabinet were from the Viceroyalty of New Spain. Smothering a grin, Gabriel quickly glanced over his shoulder. Satisfied that the scribe was still at his desk and would not interrupt, Gabriel turned back to the documents prepared to go through every single one until he found what he was looking for. Mérida was only a small part of New Spain, but he was close now. He could feel it.

# Twenty

*"...what reason have you got for going mad?"* - *Miguel de Cervantes, Don Quixote*

Jose de Beteta knocked on the door of the de Piña house promptly at 11 o'clock in the morning. After days of trying, he finally tracked down Don Ademar's lawyer and he adjusted his best doublet, feeling rather pleased with himself. He preened at his success, gleefully envisioning a promotion above the rank of simple corregidor. He knocked again, the man standing beside him waiting patiently. The door opened, and he marched inside the house without an invitation.

"I am here to see Doña Andrea de Piña," Beteta announced imperiously.

"Right this way." Recognizing him, Francisco immediately ushered them down the hallways through to the inner courtyard where Andrea sat reading a book.

She presented a pretty picture today, in a dress of pink damask silk, with a light blue lace shawl draped around her shoulders. Her hair was pulled back from her face with a matching pink ribbon, and curls fell loosely down her back. Beteta noticed none of this, tapping his foot impatiently until she noticed his presence.

Andrea looked up at the sound on the tiled floor and put her book down after carefully marking her place. She waited expectantly.

"Good morning, Doña. May I introduce Mateo Fernandez, Don Ademar's lawyer? He was hiding from me, but I, Jose de Beteta, found him."

Beteta paused as if expecting applause before gesturing to the man next to him. Andrea narrowly resisted the temptation to roll her eyes. How difficult could it be to locate one lawyer? Mateo Fernandez was a mousey looking man, with sandy hair and small, close-set eyes that darted around the room without resting on anything. His hands trembled, the whites of his knuckles showing as he squeezed them together in an attempt to stop moving. Tucked under his arm was a battered folder.

"Welcome gentlemen. Do you have any news, Corregidor Beteta?" Andrea asked.

"Ah, well, as to that -" Beteta floundered. He was a man puffed up on his own importance, and clearly not used to being questioned. He especially hated being questioned by a woman he accused of murder only days before.

"We are here to read your father's will, Doña Andrea," Fernandez interrupted, taking pity on the other man. He held out the beat-up leather folder in his arms.

"Yes, we are here about the will." Thankfulness passed over Beteta's features before his usual sneer quickly took its place. He took a seat in one of the chairs across from Andrea without waiting to be asked. He shifted uncomfortably in the metal seat before waving his hand imperiously at the lawyer. "You may begin."

Fernandez nodded and set the folder on the table after moving Andrea's book out of the way. Opening the folder, he pulled out a few pieces of paper.

"Now this is simply a formality, you understand. Will you confirm that you are Doña Andrea de Piña, daughter of Don Ademar Reynaldo de Piña?" He peered shortsightedly at Andrea as she nodded.

"Very good. Now, as requested by your father after acknowledging you as his daughter, King Felipe granted you official legitimization as a Spaniard. I have a copy of that document here. Therefore, as a Spaniard and the only living child of Don de Piña, you are his sole heir."

Andrea knew she should not be surprised. Ademar had, after all, sent for her in order to have an heir. She supposed it was the formality of it all, the lack of feeling involved. Her father was dead, and so she inherited all. Fernandez broke her reverie by handing her the papers.

"This is a list of all Don de Piña's assets. You have inherited multiple properties, including this house, as well as money and other items of value."

"Congratulations, Doña de Piña. It appears you are now a very wealthy woman," Beteta said meaningfully, his eyes narrowed. She bristled at the unspoken accusation in his voice.

"I assure you, Corregidor, I would rather have my father than his money," she responded sharply.

To Fernandez, Andrea said more calmly, "Thank you for handling my father's affairs, señor. Is there anything I need to do?"

Fernandez smiled gently at her, his eyes finally resting upon her face. "Take some time to mourn, Doña. When you are ready, I will call upon you and we can fully go over your inheritance. I will leave these for you here so that you may look at them at your leisure."

His work done, he left the papers on the table and picked up his folder, tucking it securely under his arm. Giving Andrea and Beteta a bow, he walked out of the courtyard and left the house.

Andrea waited until she heard the faint click of the front door and looked around to ensure no would overhear before turning to Beteta.

"Corregidor de Beteta, I feel I must inform you that I received a threatening note yesterday," Andrea said, taking the initiative before Beteta could hurl any more accusations at her.

"A threatening note," Beteta echoed mockingly. "And what did this threatening note say?"

"It said that I was next and that I would receive instructions on what to do." Andrea was frustrated Beteta did not seem to believe her. He looked like he was going to pat her on the head and compliment her on her imagination like she was a child, rather than a woman of twenty.

"I suppose you will just have to wait then, Doña. Meanwhile, I will continue my investigation."

Beteta stood up, the chair scraping noisily against the tile floor of the courtyard. "Good day."

Andrea closed her eyes and looked down as Beteta walked toward the door. He was maddening, absolutely maddening. She had no faith that he would be able to find her father's killer, let alone protect her from suffering the same fate. At least he

seemed to have given up on the idea that she killed her own father. Or perhaps he hadn't, though she was grateful he said nothing about it to her. Hopefully, Gabriel would be able to make
a list of men who might have known her father in Mérida and
traveled back to Spain with him. They would find the killer despite Beteta's interference and disbelief.

She thought for a moment. The killer obviously believed the
treasure was here in Sevilla, but he did not find it in the house.
She had to consider the very real possibility that the treasure was
somewhere else.

She sat in the same chair in the courtyard for hours, staring
into the distance as she sorted through all the possibilities in her
mind, looking at the list of her father's – no, her's now – properties in the hopes a likely hiding place would reveal itself. Francisco came in every so often, telling her that Don this and Doña
that were here to call upon her. She wished to receive no one,
and could not bear the thought of visitors she must put on a
show for. A hesitant cough sounded behind her, interrupting her
thoughts, and she sighed impatiently.

"I told you, Francisco, I am not at home today."

When she turned around, however, she found Gabriel, not
Francisco, standing there. At the sight of his triumphant grin,
she forgot her impatience and jumped up excitedly.

"You have the names?" she asked, practically vibrating with
eagerness. She rocked on the balls of her feet to prevent herself
from reaching towards him.

Gabriel waved a folded piece of paper in response, a huge grin
on his face. He set the list in front of her with a flourish and sat
down. He was such a contrast to Beteta who had sat there earlier

puffing off his own consequence, that Andrea immediately felt the most reassured she had since the murder. Where Beteta acted dismissive and incompetent, Gabriel was attentive and produced swift results. She picked up the paper, grinning back at him, unfolded it, and scanned the names. One, in particular, stood out amongst all the names she did not recognize: Don Sebastián de Mendoza.

"Don Sebastián!" Andrea exclaimed. "I knew it!"

Gabriel looked at her in surprise. "You suspected him?"

"He wanted me to tell him about my father's work in Mérida. That was the first anyone mentioned something like that to me, but I had almost forgotten about it."

"You forgot about it." Gabriel looked unimpressed.

"Oh I do apologize, Marqués de Silva," she dropped a low sweeping curtsey. "I was preoccupied with the fact that you were an agent of the King who only spoke to me because of his orders, and then my father was killed. I have not cared to dwell on Don Sebastián, so please forgive me," Andrea said scathingly, her face hot. How dare he judge her for this!

Gabriel immediately felt repentant. He looked at the woman, righteous with indignation sitting across from him, saw the proud tilt of her nose, the wide green eyes that just now sparkled with anger and frustration, but that recently had been clouded with fear and sadness and was moved to an apology.

"You are right. Forgive me." He would have said more, but how could he say that despite their reluctant beginning, he looked forward to seeing her every day. Even under the circumstances of murder.

"I do not know Don Sebastián well," Andrea said, letting him know she forgave him by changing the subject, "but I believe my father did. Don Sebastián came here multiple times to speak with my father in the study."

"Now we just need to find proof that he killed your father if indeed he did. We cannot accuse someone of murder without proof," Gabriel teased her. He tapped his fingers on the table. "Have you received another note?" he asked.

"No, I have not." Andrea frowned. She stood up and started to pace back and forth, her skirts swishing around her ankles. "I do not know what to do. Gabriel, I mean Marqués, I do not have the treasure! How can I tell someone else where it is if it is not here?"

She blushed over her misstep. She might refer to him as Gabriel in her thoughts, but she could not call him by his first name out loud, and he had certainly never called her by hers. She would agonize over the embarrassment later though, because she had more important things to worry about, like her life.

"What if," she continued, "the treasure is not here? What if there is no treasure at all? What do I do then?"

Following Andrea's lead, Gabriel decided to overlook the sound of his first name coming from her lips, no matter how delighted it made him feel. Trying, and failing, to keep a large smile off his face, he focused on the matter at hand.

"The king would not believe your father had the treasure here if he did not have information telling it was. Yet I believe the killer would have found the treasure if it had been hidden here in the house. Perhaps it is somewhere else in the city." He fell silent, musing over this thought.

Andrea's shoulders slumped in relief. It was indescribable

how much better she felt now that both she and Gabriel believed the treasure was not at her home. It might not truly make her safer, but she felt like it did.

"*Gracias a Dios!*" She reached out her hand impulsively toward his from where she stood. "Now if only our killer believed I do not know its location, too."

"But this makes it more difficult, don't you see?" he said, taking her hand. He squeezed it gently, before releasing it. "We still have to find the treasure. If it is not here, there are numerous places it could be hidden."

"What if someone else stole it? My father could have brought the fifth to Court and someone could have stolen it before the king received it."

Gabriel looked at her pityingly. "Unfortunately I am certain your father is the smuggler."

"I know," she sighed. She just needed to have her hope said aloud.

Walking back to the table, she picked up the documents left behind by the lawyer. "These are all the properties in my father's name. As the treasure is not here, perhaps it is at one of these?"

"Well done!" Gabriel congratulated her. "This gives us a perfect starting point. We will start our search today."

She only hoped she was right, and they would find the treasure before anything else happened.

# Twenty-One

*"Where a door is closed, another is opened." - Miguel de Cervantes, Don Quixote*

Andrea sat in the parlor awaiting Luisa. Now that the initial chaos of the murder had subsided, the household was falling into a peaceful routine, and that meant accepting more visitors. Beteta had not been back, so he either no longer suspected Andrea or he was waiting to arrest her. Andrea was grateful whatever the reason for his absence, and she ordered the study wiped clean. While Gabriel visited the first property on their list, Andrea was stuck at home. Luisa had arranged to come over to share all the gossip from the parties Andrea could not attend while in mourning.

"Your pardon, Señora," Francisco said, snapping Andrea out of her thoughts. "Doña Luisa del Toro is here to see you."

He bowed respectfully and moved aside as Luisa strode confidently into the room. She looked particularly mischievous today, in a high necked dress with small flowers delicately embroidered along the hem that did nothing to distract from the twinkle in her eye. The two friends embraced, but as Andrea opened her mouth to offer her refreshment, Luisa beat her to it.

"The Marqués de Silva asked me about you," Luisa said in her forthright way.

"Oh?" Andrea tried to appear nonchalant, busying her hands with pouring tea and stirring in sugar. She handed a teacup to Luisa, keeping her face averted. She could not say why she did not tell Luisa they were investigating Ademar's murder together, but she wanted to keep their relationship to herself even if no romance was involved.

"He seemed to know how you were doing better than I did." Luisa peered at Andrea and gasped at the latter's blushing face. "You little minx!" she laughed, playfully swatting Andrea's arm. "He is a good catch, you know. You could do much worse."

Andrea fanned her flaming cheeks. "Luisa! I have no intention of 'catching' anyone. He may have called upon me a few times, that is all. He is a very nice man."

"A very nice man," Luisa repeated, mouth open. "That is all you have to say? Has he declared himself?"

"What? Of course not," Andrea said, taken aback. "We have only known each other for a short time. He has been very kind to me and has indicated some interest, but he has done nothing to demonstrate an attachment," she finished a little sadly.

Luisa looked surprised. "No? Well, you are in mourning. He may feel you would refuse him before the mourning time is finished, or that it would be inappropriate to approach you now."

"I doubt that would stop him. More likely, he does not care for me," Andrea said, thinking how much she wished the opposite were true.

"Well have you done anything to encourage his affections?" Luisa asked.

"Not particularly," she admitted, laughing a little at Luisa's exasperated sigh.

There was, in fact, no reason for Gabriel to like her at all when she thought about it. He had sought her out because of his duty to the king and remained by her side after her father's death because his duty was not finished and he was a gentleman. It was a silly fantasy to believe he might care for her. He was a marqués and while she might be a marquesa now, she had not grown up that way. He did not love her, and she did not – would not – love him. If she repeated it often enough, she may even begin to believe it.

She did not even need to stay in Spain if she did not wish to. Without her father, there was nothing keeping her here in this foreign country. It was a beautiful country to be sure, with its courtyards and columns, but it was not home. She missed the vibrant colors of Mérida, the houses that held the obvious echo of Spain but with the added bright influence of the Maya. She missed the lush forests outside the city, the constant chatter of the birds, and the connection there she felt with her mother. Itzel's family was there, but perhaps that was the problem. She would not be allowed to return to the shop or live with them, for she was Spanish now, and they would live in completely disparate spheres. The problem was, she knew the familiar roads and plazas would no longer feel the same. She did not seem to belong anywhere.

"If you want the Marqués de Silva, you must encourage him.

You like him, do you not?" Luisa asked, regaining her friend's attention.

"I do like him, Luisa," Andrea confessed.

"There are you are then," Luisa confirmed with a smile.

Luisa did not seem to understand it was not that simple.

"I like him, but I do not know about marriage. Now that my father is gone, I do not need to stay here in Madrid. I do not even know if I want to stay here. And the marqués would never leave Spain. I could not ask it of him." Andrea was growing visibly distraught, seeing which, Luisa finally took pity on her.

"My poor friend," she said sympathetically. "I had no idea you felt this way. You have as much right to live here as anyone else. As I do. I wish you would believe me."

Andrea smiled at the girl across from her. At first glance, Luisa seemed a self-centered woman who walked through life oblivious of others around her. Andrea knew, however, that she could not have asked for a better friend.

Luisa stayed for another half hour, moving the conversation to other, more mundane topics. Once it seemed that she had forgotten about the talk of the Marqués de Silva, Luisa rose to take her leave. She left, promising to return later in the week.

Andrea remained in the parlor, sipping at her tea which had long grown cold. She would miss this house, she decided after Luisa had gone, this house, with its constant reminders of her father's family, her other family that she never known. She loved the Arabian carpets that covered the floors everywhere but the courtyard, their multicolored swirls reminding her of the ocean waves back home. She even loved Francisco and María, who had welcomed her with open arms and were taking care of her so well in Ademar's absence. She knew them better than she had known her father. If she did return to Mérida, she would try to convince them to sail across the sea and come with her. Maybe she would ask them, but not today.

* * *

Andrea ventured out of the house for the first time since her father's death that afternoon. At home, she was used to walking around by herself, but Francisco was horrified when she put her foot down and refused a maid or footman to accompany her. Ademar had never forced the issue, and now that she was on her own she could decide for herself. She snuck out when Francisco's back was turned, but she doubted she could get away with it again.

She did not mind. Andrea relished this chance to be alone, savoring the wind in her hair and the sun on her face, warming her in more ways than one. She walked along the main avenue in the center of the city, peeking into shop windows and nodding acknowledgments at the ladies and gentlemen who greeted her. The shops were filled with laces and gloves, beautiful hats, and bolts of fabrics waiting to be made into dresses. Her black mourning dress paled in comparison to the fashions of those strolling by, there to see and be seen. She wondered if those walking past her could tell she was not grieving the way she ought. After the initial shock of her father's death wore off, an emptiness had settled inside her. Ademar may have been her father, but his brief presence in her life was so peripheral that his absence had not changed her.

She paused to allow a man on a tall bay stallion to cross the street in front of her when a carriage drove past her, something pale fluttering out the side window. It was almost as if it had been thrown toward her. Andrea leaned down and picked up the paper that fell into the street. Holding it in the air, she looked around for the carriage, but it was already turning the corner ahead out of sight. Shrugging, she unfolded the paper, thinking she could return it to someone if the note was addressed. She was startled to find it was a message addressed to her.

> *Doña Andrea de Piña,*
> *You have until tomorrow morning to give up the treasure.*
> *Bring it to the Church of Santa Ana by 10 o'clock.*
> *Come alone.*

Pressing her hand against her mouth, Andrea stifled a cry and tried to regain her composure. Somehow the world continued around her. Couples walked arm in arm, and horses pulled carriages across the city. A "look alive!" from a nearby porter maneuvering a stack of hatboxes in his arms woke her up and prompted her to stuff the note in her reticule. Slightly hitching up her skirts, Andrea saw none of the bustle of the city as she hurried down the few streets home.

# Twenty-Two

*"The knight's sole responsibility is to succor them as people in need, having eyes only for their sufferings, not for their misdeeds." - Miguel de Cervantes, Don Quixote*

There was no choice. Unable to find any clues amongst her father's things, and unable to search any place other than her house the night before, she sent a message to Gabriel. As the morning went on with no reply, Andrea knew she needed to take matters into her own hands. She would walk to the church alone. Hiking her skirts up, she ran down the stairs hoping she would not see anyone. She could not have Francisco or María worry about her, and she would be unable to keep her worry from them. She managed to make it to the hallway without seeing a servant when a footman walked across the courtyard. Andrea quickly threw herself against the wall, making herself as small and invisible as possible. She held her breath until he was gone. Her chest went up and down, and she rested her hand against it to calm herself. Taking a fortifying breath, Andrea again held her skirts a little higher to walk out of the house as quickly as possible without flat out sprinting.

She rushed to the street, searching for a chaise or a carriage. She walked until she found what she searched for, two men resting leisurely against a small chaise hitched up to matching gray horses. She walked up to them with as much confidence as she could muster.

"I would like you to take me to the Church of Santa Ana." Andrea pulled a few coins out of her reticule and held them out.

Seeing the money, the men did as she hoped and pushed off against the chaise. They doffed their caps, making a production of assisting her into the chaise. Andrea sat impatiently, begging the men to hurry. They did so, encouraging the horses to a trot. Soon enough, they were driving towards the church, passing people on the street who walked by without a care in the world. With a sudden bitterness, she envied them for their lack of worry. She did not have time to stew, however, for all too soon the horses slowed and came to a stop outside a plaza. One of the men hopped down from his perch and opened the door. Without waiting for his help, she handed him the coins and jumped down.

"Thank you!" she called over her shoulder, hurrying across the plaza to the oldest church in the city.

Walking past a statue of some soldier, she walked under a beautiful granite lintel she would have stopped to admire had she not been so frightened by what was to come. She ducked inside the door and walked into the nave of the church. It was dark and empty inside, with high ceilings and tile floors that echoed with every step she took.

The bell rang 10 o'clock.

Andrea took a deep breath, wincing at the tightness in her chest. She had not slept the night before, but her tiredness was forgotten by the last peal. She walked once around the church but saw no one. After genuflecting towards the altar, she slipped into the last pew. All she could do now was wait. She bowed her head and began to pray.

He moved silently, did Don Sebastián. She never even heard him step inside the church. She did not realize what was happening until it was too late. One hand gripped her arm tightly, clenching it to the bone, while another pressed a handkerchief against her mouth. It smelled bitter with something she could not identify, and she tried to hold her breath, but her lungs protested. Within moments of breathing in, it was too late. Black crept over her vision, and her arms punched out weakly. She kicked out wildly, but he continued to hold her tightly, seemingly not feeling her blows.

It was no use. Andrea's head sagged forward and her body relaxed, her legs giving out, prompting two men to slip out of the shadows into the main body of the church. They hoisted her over one man's shoulder and covered her with a blanket before sneaking out a side door, the other man keeping watch to ensure no one saw. For a moment, Sebastián faced the altar, his usually mocking expression now replaced with something filled with malice. He made the sign of the cross, kissing his thumb to the heavens, and leisurely walked out of the church, following his henchmen to see his charge into a waiting carriage. He mounted a horse, waiting until the carriage started rambling down the street toward the edge of Sevilla before he turned his horse in the opposite direction.

\* \* \*

By the time Gabriel read Andrea's note, it was too late. His groom saddled Trueño in record time and he all but flew to the de Piña house. His hurried questions only brought a worried frown to Francisco's face. His mistress was here, surely.

Gabriel forgot his manners and pushed past Francisco to enter the house. He ran through all the rooms on the ground floor. He glanced in the study, looked in the library, checked the parlor, and walked around the courtyard into the dining room. His fear was contagious, and Francisco quickly barked orders to a nearby footman to check the Doña's bedroom. María came down the stairs minutes later, tears streaming down her face.

"The mistress is gone!" she cried.

"Gone?" He thought to Andrea's message burning a hole in his pocket. "Did she say where she was going?" he demanded. She had slipped out under the butler's nose, but maybe she had told her maid.

"She was very worried last night and this morning, Don, but she refused to tell me what was wrong. She finally said that she felt the need to pray. I do not know why she could not pray here, but she insisted."

"Where?" Gabriel asked again.

"I do not know," María sobbed. "'An old church' is all she said."

Gabriel thanked the maid over his shoulder as he rushed back out of the house. His horse was still there, being held by a lackey who came to attention as Gabriel snatched the reins and swung up into the saddle. He headed toward the center of the city without hesitation. There were many old churches, but he could not waste timing going through every old church in the city. No, he would go straight to the oldest church in Sevilla, the Church of Santa Ana.

Trueño slowed to a walk as Gabriel turned off the main street and approached the plaza in front of the church. "Whoa," he called, bringing his stallion to a stop. He whinnied and tossed his head as Gabriel threw his leg over the saddle and jumped down. He did not worry about tying the reins, but instead brought them down over Trueño's head and let them dangle. His horse rubbed Gabriel's shoulder affectionately, and Gabriel took one second of comfort before turning to run into the church. Trueño would stay put.

Gabriel slipped in through a side door, pulling it shut behind him. Andrea was not there. The nave was empty, and Gabriel allowed himself a moment of disappointment. His shoulders sagged briefly, but he shook himself. He was a Spaniard, and an agent of the king besides. Andrea was relying upon him, and he would not be sidetracked by worry. He walked up the aisle, looking down the rows of pews to see if anything had been left behind. As he reached the altar, he heard a cough. Whirling around, his hand reaching for the sword belted at his waist, he turned to find a priest exiting the confessional.

"Your pardon, *Padre*." Gabriel closed the distance between them quickly. "Have you seen anyone here, perhaps a young woman, in the last hour?"

The priest thought for a moment. "Confessions began not long ago. There was no one inside the church when I arrived, although a carriage was leaving the plaza."

"A carriage? Do you know where it was heading?"

"It was heading left down the *Calle Mayor*, but beyond that, I cannot say."

"And the carriage?" prompted Gabriel. If it headed left, that meant it was heading toward the north of the city.

"It was a simple black carriage," the priest shrugged apologetically. "I cannot say who it belonged to, for there was no crest on its doors."

Gabriel thanked the priest. It was not much to go on, but it gave him some hope he could find her. He could at least head in the right direction, and that would be enough. It had to be.

There was no time to lose. Poor Trueño was forced to abandon his mouthful of grass, as Gabriel sternly told him now was not the time. The carriage had a head start on him, and he could not bear the thought of Andrea being hurt or worse. He deftly maneuvered Trueño into the traffic of the *Calle Mayor* and headed north. He chafed at the slow pace created by the traffic but quickened to a gallop at the edge of the city. The road ahead was empty, but Andrea was there somewhere. He could feel it.

# Twenty-Three

*"...There are many hours and minutes between now and to-morrow and in any one of them – even in a minute, the house falls." - Miguel de Cervantes, Don Quixote*

It had been hours, and they were certainly on the road to Madrid, but Gabriel had finally spotted the carriage. It rolled along the road with more speed than the casual traveler, with one coachman. Gabriel stayed partially hidden by keeping his distance, but it was without a doubt the carriage carrying Andrea. "I'll be there soon," he promised to her.

The carriage was cramped. Andrea had come to with her hands tied and two dirty faces staring at her. She stiffened as one of them trailed a finger down her cheek.

"What do you think he wants her for?" he asked his partner.

"Does it matter? We have our orders." The second man leaned back, his muscles bulging as he crossed his arms.

The first man merely grinned in response. He was wirier than the other man, but no less intimidating with a long scar running his neck. It was thick and puckered, and he scratched at it absently as his eyes ran up and down Andrea's body.

She strove to hide it, but she shivered. "Where are we going?" She tried to sound tough, but given their lack of reaction, it did not work.

She tried again. "What are you going to do with me?"

When they continued to ignore her, she started whistling. If she was as annoying as possible, maybe then they would answer her. Even if they did not, she would at least be making things more difficult for them, which could only be a good thing.

The bigger man appeared unmoved, only a clench in his jaw revealing his annoyance. The other man was not so professional. His legs bounced and he glared at her, as she kept whistling, staring out the carriage window. The window had been covered in the city, but the longer they traveled, the more relaxed her captors felt, and they had drawn back the curtain some time ago.

After a particularly sharp high note, the smaller man shouted. He reached across the seat and shook her so hard her teeth rattled in her head.

"Stop that!" The first man grabbed the other and dragged him back into his seat. He pinned the man there, his words all the more forceful for being quiet. "We cannot touch her, remember? You know what happens if we do."

Moving her jaw back and forth, Andrea studied her captors. The muscled man was the one in charge, she decided. He had more control in this situation than the other man did, which made him the more dangerous.

Satisfied for now that they would not touch her, Andrea sat and planned. The men had weapons that were out of her reach, but they were there and in her line of sight. She could not do much with her hands tied, but she vowed she would not go quietly.

The sun fell in the sky as the morning passed into the afternoon. They had been on the road for hours, and they would not tell her where they were going. Don Sebastián had paid them well. She cursed him. He did not know it, based on how secretive his men were being, but she saw him at the church before she fainted. Sebastián kidnapped her, which meant he wrote her the notes and killed her father. She felt like scouring her hand with soap all over again, thinking of how he had kissed it, how he had danced with her, and called upon her with his fake sympathy.

Andrea was debated between asking more questions or starting another bout of whistling when she heard a shout and a shot. She pressed her face to the window, ignoring the men jostling behind her, and wanted to cry from relief. Gabriel had come for her.

* * *

Her face was pressed against the carriage window, eyes wide with terror. She was biting her lip, her hands pressed against the glass. He saw rope tying them together, and growled in anger. The coach had a head start on him, but he was not a good judge of horseflesh for nothing. Gabriel dug his spurs into his horse's sides. Trueño neighed indignantly, for he was already at a gallop, but his stride somehow elongated eating up the distance between him and the carriage.

Gabriel forced his stallion closer to the coach as he caught up to the back wheel. The new sound alerted the coachman, who turned around, pulling a pistol from his pocket with a shout. Gabriel had no choice but to crouch low over his reins, moving as close to the coach as he dared. The bullet whizzed over his shoulder. Well, this was certainly the right carriage, Gabriel thought wryly.

He pulled his own pistol out of its holster and took careful aim. The bullet caught the coachman square in the right shoulder. The man crumpled, dropping the reins, and fell to the side of the road. The horses continued galloping, their eyes rolling with fright. Pulling up level with the carriage now, Gabriel murmured soothingly, "Just a bit farther, Trueño."

The stallion stretched his neck forward in response. With a massive effort, Gabriel reached out to grab the flailing reins of the carriage. The horses crowded into each other in a panic, leaning away from Gabriel's horse who kept coming closer. Grasping, fingers tightening around the leather, Gabriel somehow gained control of the reins and pulled them tight.

"Whoa! Whoa there!" His horse slowed to a stop, forcing the other horses to obey his command. There was no time to check on his lady, for the carriage door was already opening. Two men jumped out, one carrying a sword, and the other a cudgel. Gabriel leaped down from his horse, with barely enough time to draw his sword before the men engaged him. He grinned, teeth gleaming in the sunlight. "En garde!"

The first man rushed forward, sword raised. He lunged first, Gabriel's sword rising to meet his in a parry. The swords clanged together, and Gabriel heard a gasp. He kept his defenses up, engaging the swordsman even as he twisted his head to glance at the carriage.

Andrea was standing there, her arm in a tight grip. The man with the cudgel was taller than Gabriel, bulky in a greatcoat so that his already large size was exaggerated, his features twisted in a sneer.

"No tricks now, Señor," the man said. "Else I might have to hurt the pretty lady."

Andrea cried out as the man painfully twisted her arm, straining the rope that tightly bound her wrists. The fight faded into the background as Gabriel looked at her, this woman who suddenly held his every hope for happiness. By God, he would not let anything happen to her. He could not.

"I will deal with you next, my dear fellow," Gabriel promised, teeth gritted.

"Look out!" Andrea shouted, looking suddenly behind him.

Gabriel turned back to meet the first man's attack. He was a good swordsman, but Gabriel was better. He parried before immediately engaging in a riposte, catching his opponent's forearm. The man grimaced, and Gabriel pressed his advantage. He sliced at the chest, and the man stumbled to his knees. Blood soaked through his shirt as his arm rested awkwardly at his side, the sword dropping out of his hand. Gabriel could not hesitate, could not observe the rules of honor, but he did not want to kill. Yet.

He needed information. He kicked away the man's sword and swung his left fist with all his strength. The punch caught the man under the chin, and he fell backward unconscious.

With a commendable lack of hesitation, the other man

pushed Andrea away from him, ready to rush Gabriel. She stumbled, but quickly righted herself.

"Get back in the carriage," Gabriel shouted, not waiting to see if she listened to him. He needed her out of harm's way so he could focus.

As it was, Gabriel jumped out of the way of the cudgel, barely missing his sword arm. Gabriel circled the big man, reaching out with his sword to test the man's defenses. It was awkward, dueling sword to cudgel against the bigger man. He was not fast, but he was strong. Gabriel grimaced as the cudgel glanced off his thigh. The man had a longer reach, but Gabriel had a greater desire to win, and so he ignored the pain, forcing himself to keep all of his body weight on both legs. He took a firmer grasp on the hilt of his sword.

"Who hired you?" Gabriel asked, lunging his sword at the man's shoulder.

It had worked against the other man, so he hoped his luck would hold. The man merely grunted as the tip of the sword sliced through the greatcoat but did not cut the flesh. Gabriel disengaged and tried again.

"Who hired you?"

This time his thrust made his mark, cutting a tendon in the man's arm. It hanged limply and the man moved the cudgel to his other hand, but Gabriel was too fast. He leaped forward, sword point the man's throat. He pulled out his gun, also pointing it at the man's head. The big man seemed to crumble before him, no longer quite so big or fierce.

"I asked you a question. Who hired you?"

The man raised his uninjured arm in a gesture of surrender. "I never knew his name, Señor. I just do what I'm told. He said to take the girl, so I take the girl."

Gabriel tried a different track as he slipped the gun back into his pocket, keeping his sword ready just in case. "If you do not know who he is, what did he look like?"

"He dressed like you, Señor, but he was shorter. When he first said what he wanted, I thought he joking. He kept smiling, but he did not seem happy. He did not like mixing with us common folk in the dirt, *sabe*?

Gabriel did understand, and he did not like killing. So he said, "Be off with you, now. And do not let me see you again. Take your friend with you."

The man nodded quickly and scrambled to his feet. He gathered up his partner who was slowly waking up on the ground, and they limped off. Not bothering to look after them, Gabriel wiped his sword on the grass and sheathed it, his suspicion of who was behind Andrea's kidnapping growing. He looked up as the carriage door swung open. Andrea descended the steps quickly, all but throwing herself into his arms.

"Gabriel, oh Gabriel," she cried.

Gabriel brought his arms around her shaking shoulders. He hesitated, then rested his cheek against her hair, breathing deeply.

"I have never been so afraid, Gabriel. Oh, how I prayed you would come for me." Andrea buried her face in his chest.

"Did they hurt you?" He demanded, putting her at arm's length so he could see her face.

"Not really." Andrea shuddered remembering the horror of waking up in a carriage being stared at by the two men, before grinning suddenly. "I think I hurt them worse than they hurt me."

Gabriel tilted his head at her questioningly.

"I whistled incredibly off-key for an unbearably long time."

He could not help the laugh that escaped him at how proud she looked. "What a warrior you are," he looked down at her fondly. "I know you may not trust me yet, *querida*, but I do hope you know that I, that I care about what happens to you."

She could not help a moment of irritation when Gabriel said he cared what happened to her. She wanted him to do more than just care. The rescue was lovely, but he could not know how she longed to hear a declaration of love. But how nice it was to be called *querida*. Because she did trust him. She more than trusted him. She loved him. She knew that now with certainty. But, she told herself sternly, now was not the time to discuss feelings.

"What will happen now, Gabriel?" Andrea asked, looking up into his eyes.

"First we should untie your hands." The knot was too tight to undo, so he reached down into his boot and withdrew the knife sheathed there and very carefully sawed through the bindings. He rubbed her wrists to help her circulation, noting with dismay the redness and marks left behind by the rope.

"And now I will take you home where you will be safe."

"And you?"

"I will find the carrion who did this to you, and kill him," Gabriel said fiercely.

"It was Don Sebastián. He snuck up behind me at the Church of Santa Ana," she said, confirming his suspicions. "But I do not see why I have to go home," Andrea continued hotly. "I was the one kidnapped. I am not the sit quietly and do nothing type."

Gabriel laughed at her mulish expression. "No, you are not. But these men have already hurt you. I cannot, I will not risk that happening again."

Andrea had to admit, if only to a very secret part of herself, that Gabriel had a point. She had been kidnapped once already, and she was not in the mood to be kidnapped again. Being drugged was not an experience she cared to repeat. However, Sebastián had involved her father and now her, and she would not do nothing.

"I can at least do something, even if I cannot duel," she insisted.

"Certainly, but please do it at home."

Andrea had the whole ride back to the city to convince Gabriel otherwise, so she conceded the battle for now. Gabriel led her over to Trueño who had, with the serenity of animals, occupied himself by munching on grass during the duel. He knelt and held out his cupped hands to received Andrea's boot. With as much dignity as she could muster, she allowed him to help her mount.

"I apologize for the lack of sidesaddle," Gabriel said as he mounted up behind her. "This was not what I envisioned when I offered to teach you how to ride horses."

"You mean you did not plan for this to happen?" Andrea teased.

She hesitated briefly before deciding to take advantage of her current situation and leaning back in his arms, which tightened around her in response. It was all deliciously improper. She supposed something would have to be done about the skirts that settled somewhere around her calves before people surrounded them, but for now, there was no one around for miles. She sighed contentedly, entwining her hands in the horse's mane as Trueño wheeled around back towards Sevilla, and set off at a steady canter.

# Twenty-Four

*"There is no recollection which time does not put an end to, and no pain which death does not remove." - Miguel de Cervantes, Don Quixote*

The moon was rising by the time they reached the de Piña house in Sevilla. The door opened as Gabriel lifted Andrea down from the horse. She stretched her legs, wobbling unevenly from the time spent in a saddle, so Gabriel kept a tireless arm around her shoulders, supporting her through the front door opened by a startled Francisco.

"I will have refreshments sent to the parlor, Marqués de Silva," Francisco murmured, whose surprise gave way to visible relief. He jerked into action, summoning someone to take Gabriel's horse, and maids to fetch food and drink from the kitchen.

Gabriel nodded and continued escorting Andrea inside. He helped her to a couch before he, too, sat down with a thankful sigh. He had had an easier time of it than Andrea, but he could no longer ignore the pain in his thigh. He rubbed at what would most likely turn into a florid bruise, as Francisco opened the door. A housemaid entered carrying a tray laden with sandwiches, pastries, and tea. Gabriel filled a plate and carried it over to Andrea.

"You should eat something," he said.

Andrea picked up a sandwich and took a bite, realizing she had not eaten all day. "I feel very silly to be so tired all of a sudden," she said, swallowing a large bite. "I do not know what you must think of me."

"I believe kidnapping is a good excuse for tiredness," Gabriel replied, trying to keep a straight face. He could not resist a chuckle, however, as Andrea took another bite of her sandwich and chewed with her eyes closed.

"I suppose," she allowed after a while.

They sat like that in silence together for a while, neither knowing how to put into words what they both desperately wanted to say. Andrea succeeded first.

"Thank you, Gabriel," she hesitated before adding, "I am very glad it was you who found me."

She set her plate down and suddenly met his eyes. "It is not true you know, not anymore. I do trust you."

Gabriel smiled. He moved over to the couch to sit next to Andrea, and took her hand, pulling it into his lap. Her fingers trembled with nerves and she looked at him, for once unsure of what was going to happen next. He stared blankly at their hands a moment before all his hesitation melted away.

"I cannot begin to tell you how I felt when I read your note," he began. "I rushed here to the house, but you were already gone.

It was as though the ground had been pulled out from under me. I would not have rested until I found you."

Andrea's eyes burned as he drew ever closer. She held her breath, instinctively knowing he was going to kiss her. Her eyes fluttered closed, and she felt his breath on her face. She suddenly felt caged and could not breathe, and belatedly realizing they must still track down Sebastián, she fluttered and pulled away.

Cheeks aflame, Andrea stammered, "What, what will happen when Don Sebastián realizes I am no longer kidnapped?"

She plucked nervously at her skirts, looking anywhere but at the man trying not to appear crestfallen beside her. "The men I was with, they said he was to meet us wherever we were going," she said miserably.

Gabriel bit back a sigh and pushed away the rejection. He turned toward her. "What did Don Sebastián intend to do with you?"

It struck him as odd that Sebastián was not in the carriage when he had found Andrea, especially if they were fleeing the city.

"I saw him only briefly," Andrea explained. "It is all a bit hazy, but I think he was going to force me to give him the treasure. That way he would get his money."

"His money?" Gabriel asked sharply. "Why do you say it like that?"

She was surprised at his intensity. "That's what those men said before they knew I was awake."

Gabriel leaned forward, his elbows resting on his knees, his brow furrowed in thought. Nodding off in the silence, Andrea jerked to attention when he stood up with a triumphant shout.

"That's it!"

He pulled a bewildered Andrea to her feet and twirled her around as if in a dance. Caught up in his excitement, Andrea found herself wrapped in his arms, confused but certain she was about to receive some good news. Gabriel pulled her to his chest and looked down at her, the laughter fading gradually from his eyes.

"I understand now, *querida*."

For he knew exactly where Sebastián would be, and he finally understood what this whole mess was really about.

"I must go. Send for the Corregidor and tell him to meet me at the palace to arrest Don Ademar's killer."

"Now?"

"Yes, it cannot wait. Don Sebastián will not wait, so neither can we."

By now Gabriel and Andrea were inches apart. She opened her mouth to protest her limited role in the upcoming capture and arrest of her own father's killer, not to mention her kidnapper when Gabriel bent his head and silenced her with a kiss. It was all too brief, really just a light brushing of lips, but there was work still to be done.

Gabriel grinned at the stunned girl and overrode the temptation to stay and kiss her again, this time properly.

"I will be back soon," he promised, " and I will come to collect *my* treasure."

With the hint of a wink and another smile, he was gone, leaving Andrea standing there still in shock.

# Twenty-Five

*"Bear in mind, Sancho, that one man is no more than another, unless he does more than another." - Miguel de Cervantes, Don Quixote*

While Andrea pushed all thoughts of romance from her mind to deal with Beteta, Gabriel rode toward the palace, grin firmly in place. The white plaster columns of the Alcázar rose before him. He could not stop, as he usually did, to admire the balustrade, but he felt the approving eyes of the saints and long-dead kings atop the facade. They bolstered his strength as he ran past a lackey, throwing the front door open himself, leaving Trueño behind.

He had been to the palace many times before and knew his way around. He did not wish to go straight to Felipe without Sebastián in tow, so he started searching rooms one at a time, lackeys and footmen trailing behind him calling for him to stop. Ignoring them, Gabriel continued to search for the man he should have realized all along was responsible. After a fruit-less search of the ground floor, Gabriel reached the Royal Pharmacy, a recent addition to the palace. There, searching frantically amongst the many jars of medicines and tinctures was Sebastián. The physician was nowhere to be found.

Gabriel leaned casually against the door, not bothering to close it. He wanted an audience for what was about to happen.

"Hello, Don Sebastián."

Sebastián jumped, clearly startled. He looked up, a cruel twist to his mouth and narrowed eyes, glaring as he recognized the voice.

"You," he growled.

Glass jars clanked together as Sebastián added one to the already crowded shelf. He started forward, hand on his sword threateningly.

"Really, Sebastián, here where anyone can find us? You should really reconsider, my dear fellow."

He spoke casually, but all the while he was drawing forth his own sword. It rested at his side, ready for the inevitable moment when Sebastián leaped forward, sword upraised in an attack.

Gabriel pushed himself off the door and swung his sword up, meeting Sebastián's with a reverberating clang. The two men circled each other, testing the other's skill. It was a grim fight, and both men soon breathed heavily. Gabriel might have had the advantage in skill, but he had fought once, and been injured, already today and Sebastián was fresh and spoiling for a fight. The din would raise the alarm, and someone would reach them soon. Gabriel had someone waiting for him, and he would win so he could return to her. This would have to be fought carefully though, he realized as he pulled his sword arm short. A fight like this could only end in a confession. There would be no quick ends today.

With any luck, Beteta would arrive at the palace soon, and at least Andrea was safe at home. And so Gabriel teased Sebastián, pressing his defenses, delaying, not pursuing the advantage.

Sebastián was no mean swordsman, but it was all he could do to hold Gabriel at bay. He cried out in frustration. "What do you want, cur!"

Gabriel beat away a parry, just north of sloppy. "I want you to confess. You killed Don Ademar. What did he do? Tell you he had no treasure?"

Sebastián snarled. "The stupid man sent his prize on a different ship. I nearly strangled him when our fleet was attacked and the ship sank." His thrusts went wild.

"Why did you care? You had become wealthy in the New World." Gabriel tried to look as though this news was not a surprise, but inside he reeled. He assumed Sebastián stole the treasure before it entered Spain, and now to learn it was lost at sea! His whole mission had been based on faulty information. No one had known the treasure was irrecoverable.

"Don Ademar accumulated wealth beyond even my wildest imaginings." Sebastián looked at Gabriel as though he could not believe his naïveté. "I wanted it. It belonged to me. I did his dirty work in New Spain while he was here, doing nothing. I was the one who did the actual labor for the government. Me! Why should he get all the reward? Why should he get to keep what I collected? All because my family is not as rich, as powerful? No. It was mine by right. Our good King is already bankrupt. One less fifth would not have made a difference."

Sebastián frothed at the mouth, his hatred for Ademar running far deeper than Gabriel could have guessed. Gabriel could now hear footsteps running up the hallway toward the pharmacy. Reinforcements at last. He lunged at Sebastián, pushing him toward the other end of the room, away from the door.

Careful not to knock into any of the tables lined up in rows, he continued pressing his advantage, forcing Sebastián backward. The footsteps stopped outside the door, and Gabriel knew he had his witness. It was time to make an end.

"Why did you kill Don Ademar?"

Sebastián wiped his forehead, struggling now to block the attack of Gabriel's flashing sword. He was slowing down. "His precious daughter was expected and stood to inherit all. All," he spit out. "With Don Ademar out of the way, I could take the girl, marry her, and make her give up her fortune to me."

Servants and noblemen alike were gathering just outside the pharmacy door, drawn by the shouts and clashes of swords. Guards pushed their way to the front, stopping short at the sight of the fight. They stood there, hushed, unable to interfere without causing a fatal lapse in concentration.

Ready now to make an end, Gabriel feinted left, before attacking right in the blink of an eye. The sword clattered out of Sebastián's hand, falling to the floor. Sebastián gaped, looking at his sword as though it, too, had betrayed him. He turned and ran to the shelves he was at before. Gabriel followed close behind him.

"It is over now, Sebastián," he called. He gestured to the door, his other arm pointing his sword unwaveringly at Sebastián.

"With these men as my witness, I have heard your confession, and I will bring you before the judge to answer for your crime."

Sebastián's chest rose and fell rapidly, looking panicked for the first time as the inevitable conclusion played out before him. His eyes darted to the rows of jars a split second before he sprang into action. He moved jars and containers around on the shelf, panicked, looking for the one he placed there before the duel. He held it up to the light, considering. Inside the jar was a clear liquid, sloshing around.

"No," Sebastián said quietly, his words all the more intense because of his calm. "No, I will not be handed over."

Sebastián unscrewed the lid and put the jar to his mouth without hesitation.

Gabriel's sword dropped to the floor unheeded as he leaped toward Sebastián. He knocked the jar out of Sebastián's hands, but it was too late. Sebastián already swallowed a mouthful. Almost immediately, he fell, writhing in pain.

Gabriel knelt down, checking Sebastián's pulse. "Find the physician! Hurry," he shouted towards the door. His shout awoke the stunned group and someone took off running down the hallway.

"No, no, no," Gabriel moaned as Sebastián clutched at his throat. It could not end this way.

Someone pushed Gabriel out of the way, and a physician knelt over Sebastián, a bulging bag at his feet.

"Hold him down," the doctor ordered.

Gabriel knelt, pressing Sebastián's shoulders down into the floor as the doctor fumbled with Sebastián's ruff. The doctor then tried to pull off the doublet, but it was too stiff and Sebastián was still writhing, thrashing wildly.

"Here."

Gabriel pulled a small knife from his boot and slashed the doublet down the middle. The physician stared at him.

"Come on, man. Heal him," Gabriel demanded.

The physician snapped out of his stupor and resumed his work. He quickly opened Sebastián's shirt and pressed his ear against the sick man's chest listening to the heartbeat. He pursed his lips and turned to the bag next to him.

Rifling through his kit, the physician pulled out a linen bag and extended a hand for Gabriel's knife. He reached into the bag and took out a small bezoar. Eyes narrowed in concentration, he carefully sliced a small strip from the bezoar. Gabriel watched as he took a small jar filled with some kind of liquid, and mixed it with the bezoar strip.

"Lift him up," the physician said, stirring the contents of the jar together.

Sebastián's convulsions had weakened by this time, and Gabriel supported his almost dead weight. Gabriel shifted, freeing one hand to pry open Sebastián's mouth. The doctor took over from there, pouring the contents of the jar down Sebastián's throat. He pressed Sebastián's mouth closed, forcing him to swallow.

The doctor leaned back. "Lay him on his side."

Gabriel did so, asking, "Will he live?"

"Only time will tell."

# Twenty-Six

*"To dream the impossible dream, that is the quest." - Miguel de Cervantes, Don Quixote*

Everything happened quickly after that. Corregidor Beteta arrived, as did his sergeants. Statements were taken, and Gabriel dutifully recited Sebastián's confession, thankfully corroborated by the footman first on the scene. With a 'hmmph' and some messily scribbled notes, Beteta begrudgingly accepted the outcome of the duel. He could do no less in front of the many spectators. The official record would show the Don Sebastián killed Don Ademar. It was enough, and it was over.

The Duque of Alba stopped Gabriel on his way out of the Pharmacy. Impatient to be gone, he allowed the somber duque leave to inform Felipe of the treasure's fate, saying that he would return to court at a later time to fill in the details. Grumbling at the whims of youth, the Duque reluctantly permitted Gabriel to leave the palace. After hours of telling the same story over and over again, Gabriel once more sat astride Trueño and guided him toward his lady's house.

He found her seething with impatience, fretting at her forced inactivity and pacing holes into the carpets. Gabriel propped himself against a doorway, the action familiar but this time looking at a very different, infinitely more pleasing sight.

"It is done, Andrea," he said.

She stopped abruptly, hands dropping to her sides as she stared at him, hesitating to believe him. "Don Sebastián?"

"Under arrest."

"He confessed?" she gasped.

He nodded. "We fought and he confessed it all."

He would have continued, but Andrea interrupted him, racing towards him. Her hands checked over him, touching his arms, his chest, his stomach, looking for any injuries.

"Peace!" Gabriel chuckled. He stopped her roving hands, holding them firmly in his grasp. "I am as you see, unharmed."

Andrea gazed up at him, speechless. She could not know how her eyes said what her mouth could not. She saw only a beloved face looking down at her, strong hands holding hers. Drawing a shaky breath, the day's events caught up to her.

"I am so relieved that you are safe, Marqués de Silva," she said lamely, her courage failing her. She held herself still.

"Do you not think we might continue to use each other's first names?" he asked wistfully.

"It does seem rather silly, does it not?" she agreed, laughing. "We have been through so much, in such a short time, and yet I should not be alone with you. This is most improper, Gabriel." Andrea's mouth curved into an impish grin, more at ease with this lighthearted teasing.

She turned her head to look pointedly at the closed door but made no move to leave Gabriel's arms. In fact, she intended to remain there quite comfortably for the foreseeable future.

Her arms moved up toward Gabriel's neck without her telling them to, and she leaned back to better peer at his face. His arms encircled her waist, pulling her in closer, tighter. This time she felt no shyness or hesitation, deciding to trust that she did not imagine the love that must have motivated his every action that day.

"I had thought to return to New Spain," she began slowly, "but now I seem to think it may be better to remain here instead. I have not decided though. I have no more family here, you see." Here her newfound poise deserted her.

Andrea lowered her eyes, flushing slightly. "What do you think?"

"Only this," Gabriel bent his head and gently touched his lips to hers.

Andrea sighed into his mouth, softening. Gabriel's arms tightened around her. But before he could deepen the kiss, someone knocked softly on the door.

Gabriel cursed under his breath, but let his arms drop. Andrea stood there, eyes closed, a flush still dusting her cheeks. Her eyes fluttered open and she smiled at him.

Seeing her standing there, so lovely and trusting, it took all his willpower to not kiss her again. "We will continue this later," he promised, delighting in her deeper blush.

Thankfully Francisco opened the door before he could do anything foolish.

"Doña Luisa del Toro," Francisco announced.

* * *

Luisa swept inside the parlor with a flurry of skirts, pushing past Francisco who bowed with a commendably straight face. For once she wore muted colors, the lack of adornment and low cut neckline at once innocent and suggestive.

"Have you heard?" she asked, before quickly embracing Andrea and sitting down. She did not once look at Gabriel.

"Heard what?" Andrea replied, looking at Gabriel who looked equally confused. Surely Luisa did not know about the duel. Word did not spread that quickly. But she was wrong.

Luisa leaned forward. "Don Sebastián has been arrested," she announced dramatically.

Andrea gasped obligingly. Sneaking a glance at Gabriel, she saw him peering intensely at Luisa, his eyes narrowed and a thoughtful frown on his face. Andrea's mind raced as she scrambled for something innocuous to say.

It took too long. Luisa's shrewd eyes narrowed, one eyebrow arched in deliberate question. After what seemed an age, Gabriel broke the silence.

"Is that so?" he asked, his tone polite but disinterested.

If Luisa was disappointed by the lack of reaction, she hid it well, except for a lightning-quick flash of irritation in her eyes. She blinked, and in its place was her normal excitement for gossip.

"Yes," Luisa agreed, "it seems Don Sebastián has been up to no good for some time." She turned to Andrea, her lips drooping with sympathy. There may have even been a tear, but that could have been a trick of the light. "My dear, Don Sebastián killed your father."

Taking her cue from Gabriel, Andrea did not let on that she already knew about Sebastián. Putting her fledgling skills of deception to work, she adopted a dismayed expression.

"He, what? Don Sebastián? How do you know this?" Andrea's hand fluttered near her heart in a show of distress, not entirely faked.

Perhaps she had acted over the top though because she heard a swiftly stifled chuckle from Gabriel. Luisa looked between the two of them.

"I just cannot believe it. Are you certain?" Andrea asked quickly before Luisa could grow more suspicious than she already appeared.

It seemed to satisfy her. Luisa leaned back in her chair.

"I am certain, Andrea. I have it on good authority that Don Sebastián confessed earlier today. I am only sorry that I must be the one to tell you, my very dear friend. Do you have any idea why he might have done such a terrible thing?"

Luisa had been a good friend to Andrea, her only friend really, since her arrival in Spain, but something about this visit began to ring false. Andrea knew her friend loved to gossip, but this entire conversation felt forced, and she was used to getting along so easily with Luisa. Luisa's eyes darted around the room searching for something, although for what Andrea did not know.

After a long pause, Andrea spoke.

"I cannot say why Don Sebastián hurt my father. They had

business together, but you know how private my father was. He never told me anything."

"Perhaps a business deal went poorly," Gabriel suggested.

Andrea nodded in agreement.

"Yes, yes, perhaps you are right," Luisa said slowly. She took a calculated pause, then with a sly glance at Gabriel said, "I shall take my leave of you. I have interrupted your grief for long enough, I simply wanted you to know about Don Sebastián."

"Oh," Andrea stood hurriedly as Luisa rose from her seat. "Of course, Luisa. Thank you for coming to see me. It is good to know, now, that I can put all this behind me."

She stepped forward to embrace Luisa as was their custom.

Luisa bared her teeth in a smile, returning the hug more tightly than was warranted. "You are a very good sort of girl, Andrea. It would be such a shame if something were to happen to you."

Gabriel watched, horrified, as Luisa backed against the door, pulling Andrea with her. With one fluid movement, Luisa pulled a knife from her reticule and put it up to Andrea's neck. She glared at him as he made to follow. He put his hands up in a pleading motion.

"Luisa, what are you doing?" Andrea's eyes were wide, and she gulped, the knife nicking her neck with a sting.

Gabriel saw red at the thin trickle of blood that appeared, and he made to step forward.

"Ah, ah," Luisa said mockingly, pointing the knife at him. "I'll have none of that now."

Gabriel stopped, letting out a breath as Luisa returned the blade to Andrea. The point dug into her skin.

"What is this about Doña Luisa?" Gabriel kept his voice light and held still as she watched him carefully.

"You killed him," she sobbed. "You killed my Sebastián."

Andrea wanted to shout that Sebastián killed her father first, but she was not willing to antagonize a woman with a knife to her throat.

"I thought Don Sebastián had been arrested," Andrea said instead.

"He was, but then he died. And you killed him," she screamed at Gabriel, curls falling out her coiffure with each jerky movement. The knife dug a little deeper.

"Sebastián drank poison. I saw the physician try to help him, Luisa, but there was nothing more he could do."

"No, I was there!" Luisa began to sob, her arm loosening around Andrea's shoulders.

Andrea did not draw attention to it, but Gabriel noticed. He kept talking, taking small steps forward.

"If you were there, then you know Sebastián planned to marry Andrea," he said, ignoring the sharp look of surprise Andrea darted at him.

Luisa scoffed. "Only for her money. He loved me." Her hold loosened even more as she directed her ire toward Gabriel.

"Perhaps." Gabriel stepped closer, the women nearly within reach.

"No, he loved me, he was going to marry me," she protested, tears pouring down her face. She wiped at them angrily with the hand holding the knife.

Taking the opportunity, Andrea wrenched herself out of Luisa's grasp. Gabriel grabbed her and thrust her behind him.

"*Querida*, look for something we can use to bind her hands," he said, keeping his eyes on Luisa. She was crying against the door, rocking back and forth, the knife forgotten in her hands.

He took the knife carefully out her grasp, handing it to Andrea to put down when she gave him a curtain tie back. He deftly tied Luisa's hands together and guided her to a chair. She sat, silently weeping.

"Go find Francisco and have him find Beteta. I will stay and watch her," he told Andrea, who was staring at her former friend.

Andrea shook her head. "No, I will watch her. I want to talk to her."

She gave him a small smile when he only stood there. "I will be fine."

Gabriel nodded, and with one last tug of the bindings to be sure they were secure, he went in search of Francisco.

With the knowledge that Beteta could not be far away, he returned to the parlor to find the women exactly as he had left them. They sat there in silence until Beteta arrived, one sergeant in tow. They would take Luisa home, placing her under guard until Andrea decided what to with her. But there would be time for that later.

"Is it truly over this time?" Andrea asked tiredly some time later.

"Unless you have something to confess?" Gabriel asked.

She smiled shyly, shaking her head. "Do you?"

"No, but I do have a request," Gabriel said, walking over to the couch Andrea sat on. He sat down as she looked at him expectantly. "Stay. Stay here in Spain, with me."

He need not have been nervous, for he found her answer in

the way her entire face lit up. Nothing else needed to be said. He poured his love for her, his hope for the future, and all his frustrations, into his kiss. Gabriel had found something better than gold trinkets or accolades from the king. He had found something infinitely more valuable, and all the more to be treasured. And now that she was safe in his arms, he would never let her go.

# Acknowledgements

I would like to thank my family and friends for their unwavering support and encouragement throughout the writing and publication process. This book would not be here without them.

To my father - the title of this book is in no way a reflection of you. To my mother, thank you for your gentle words the first time I was brave enough to share my manuscript with you. To my editors and early readers, thank you for polishing this story into something ready for consumption. To Beetiful Book Covers, thank you for designing the most beautiful book cover.

And to you, the reader. Thank you for purchasing and reading this novel. Your support means the world to me.

Mia got her start filling notebook after notebook with loops she called cursive. As a Mexican American, she dreamed of stories with a Mexican heroine but could not find exactly what she was looking for, so she decided to write her own stories. Mia has a Bachelor's degree in History and Medieval Studies from the University of Notre Dame and a Master's degree in Education from Boston University. She currently lives in England with her husband and adorable puppy. This is her first novel.